MW01148251

CALOOSAHATCHEE

by

Toby Benoit

1663 Liberty Drive, Suite 200
Bloomington, Indiana 47403
(800) 839-8640
www.authorhouse.com

This book is a work of fiction. Places, events, and situations in this story are purely fictional and any resemblance to actual persons, living or dead, is coincidental.

First published by AuthorHouse 08/02/04

ISBN: 1-4184-7548-3 (sc)

Printed in the United States of America
Bloomington, Indiana

This book is printed on acid-free paper.

I

It was over! He had known that one day he'd hear the news. At least he prayed to live long enough to hear it. His name was Carter and every day that passed since he had joined the fight for secession, had found him praying to hear the war was over and now it was. A dispatch rider wearing a tattered gray overcoat despite the Summer heat, rode along the ranks of the weary men shouting the news out loud. No one celebrated. Each man stood with his own thoughts, hollow eyed and ragged, quietly absorbing the moment.

Slowly, Carter turned the words over in his mind. He needn't ask who won for the entire Confederate army had been living in defeat for the last year, hanging on to their pride and the hope that once again they might rally behind the old general and regain some of that swagger they'd known in the good times. Oh those noble times when they had marched the fields with honor, glory and victory making it known that the southern people would not allow Mr. Lincoln's army to linger south of the Potomac. Then there had been Gettysburg and Sherman's march to the sea. Now the conquest was complete and the Confederate army had been beaten. There hadn't been any doubt to the outcome in recent times for Carter and his brothers in arms had been marching for months on mostly bare feet and empty stomachs through the once fertile farmlands of Ol' Dixie. Now, the general had conceded defeat and news of his surrender was spreading like a brush fire.

The old general was Robert E. Lee. Carter had seen the man only once during his year of service and was still in awe of the man. The old fellow had a reassuring confidence about him that so motivated the soldiers he led. It had been the dawn of Carter's first battle while he was facing the inevitable doubts that a soldier will always face at such a time. They had formed ranks and were preparing an assault across a mile of open ground through a hail of cannon and into the face of the entrenched Yankee army. As they awaited the orders to advance the grandfatherly old general rode along the column of soldiers offering a word of prayer and envoking each man to seek his own peace with the Lord and replacing fear in men's hearts with courage and determination. As the general rode past Carter, he spoke in a loud clear voice to them all while his face beamed with pride in his troops and his old eyes flashed bright. Carter knew certainly that this man before him was less than a god, but surely he was more than any man.

By the time the general had made his way through the ranks, there wasn't a soldier among them who wasn't ready to fight. Then at the dropping of a sword and the ringing of the bugle, Carter and his comrades numbering many thousands, began their march across that little Pennsylvania field. They marched into the face of the devil himself unflinchingly for the South, their families and for that dashing fellow who had so inspired them. It was nearly the fourth of July, he recalled. The nearest town was named Gettysburg. That battle lasted three days and claimed over sixty thousand casualties combined. It began the war for Carter and the end of the war for the South. The sights, sounds, smells and fear he encountered those few days left him feeling empty, not quite whole anymore. He'd survived untouched by bullets or sword, yet he had been touched and the empty feeling followed him throughout the rest of the war. It was that emptiness that he was feeling now as the news of surrender lay on his mind. He wanted to celebrate, but couldn't. He wanted to kneel and pray, but somehow had forgotten how. He wanted to cry, to mourn those lost, but somewhere over the miles marched, he had lost that privilege. Instead, Carter took a seat beneath the shade of a lightning scarred hickory, among many of his comrades and echoed their silence.

The detachment would remain together for awhile yet, until orders could come through officially releasing them from their duties and instructing them as to what should be expected of them as members of the defeated army. Soon he would be a free man again. Free to return to the home he hadn't seen in so long. Free to return to the loved ones he so sorely missed. But first, there was to be a protocol expected to be followed by all surrendering troops and he would follow it to the letter. Now, however was no time for thoughts of home and freedom. Now, wasn't time for him to review what had been lost or what gain the future may hold. Now he simply wanted to sit in the shade of that old hickory tree and just know it was over. Planning and reflection would come later. At this time, just knowing it was enough.

Once the news had arrived, the captain had ordered a rest from the days march which had been underway for some time and after an hour or more in the shade, Carter hear the assembly sounding from the bugler. The timy blasts echoed down the line of weary men and slowly they clambered to their feet. Carter uncoiled his six feet tall body and placing his gray cap back upon his unruly shock of blonde hair, reclaimed his place in the column of march and listened to the dull murmurings and clink and clang of equipment as the others gained their positions and awaited the signal to advance. As they moved out he gave notice to the rhythmic pounding of many feet and the grunts and sighs of men under burden when a mild voice reached his ear, singing quite lovely, the Battle Hymn of the Republic. As they continued their march through the devastated countryside, wearing their torn and tattered garments which showed little resemblance to uniforms, their bare feet kicked up the dry dust of the Georgia dirt road and the song spread from that one frail voice to a regular chorus as many others joined in. Carter didn't join the song, but it did bring out a thin smile to his face. Defeated? Not entirely.

Clouds had began to form up and thunder sounded in the West as the column halted and the orders spread for each man to prepare himself for a nights rest and what meager rations he could come by. Many lines of smoke were showing on the not too distant horizon as Carter erected his tarp for a rain shelter and managed to get beneath it as best he could. At six feet and two inches both feet stuck out from the back of his make shift shelter and his blonde hea stuck out from the other end. And in time the rain began. The storm wasn't bad at all and provided a nice steady shower which many of his fellows readily took advantage of by stripping off their clothes and enjoying the first real bath many of them had enjoyed in a very long time.

The night came on and the rains passed as Carter lay beneath his tarp alone, listening to the muffled conversations of men about him as they talked of what was to come and each offering his own set of predictions for his listeners to contemplate. He tried to sleep, but sleep was always hard won, so he lie as he usually did, remembering home. He thought of Ma and Pa and his brother Seth all waiting for him to come home. He would always picture Ma in the kitchen, where she spent most of her time, lovingly preparing the most wonderful of meals to keep her family fed and strong. He thought of Pa in the hay field or tending the peach orchard and at night reading the old leather-bound Bible while insisting the boys learn their verses. He thought of Seth, his older brother by a couple of years, who had left home at the onset of the war only to return shortly afterward, having been wounded and in no shape to fight. He thought of farming and being a farmer. Remembering the feel of the plow in his hands and the satisfying ache in his shoulders after a day of planting, weeding, watering and harvesting. Of swinging Pa's old claw hammer repairing fences, gates and other odd jobs. He'd spent countless nights in this manner trying to find sleep, letting his mind dwell on home and not the horror. He believed if he thought of the carnage he'd experienced too often, he surely would lose his mind.

Carter rose from his soggy bed beneath his tarp in time to watch the troops being awakened. The officers of the company were going from man to man shaking them awake without the aid of the bugle. As they did they offered words of encouragement and kindness to the soldiers. Carter was already stowing his tarp and bedroll on his pack as his captain approached and Carter greeted him with a smart salute. The salute was returned as the captain spoke.

"It's getting near time for us to be breakfasting and breaking camp. We'll be getting on the move again soon. There's a Yankee camp about a mile and a half down the road and we'll be heading over there this morning to surrender our arms. How's your spirits holding up son?"

"I suppose I could be feelin' a bit better than I am, but all things considered, I guess I'm alright. Any Idea what them bluebellies got in store for us today sir? Will we be allowed to go home soon?"

"Well private, I don't rightly know as I can answer that. If I could, I'd be a right comfortable man, but I can't. I did speak with the major last night and he doesn't know yet himself, but he did say, however, that no matter what does take place, he wants us all to conduct ourselves as gentlemen. The war's over, the fighting's behind us, so don't let them gall you into acting out. Is that clear?"

"Yessir Cap'n, I'll be fine." Carter assured the man and reaching out his hand he spoke. "Thanks to you Cap'n. I've been honored to serve under you." The captain returned Carter's grip firmly and nodded his thanks then slowly turned away to awaken more of the still slumbering soldiers.

After what meager breakfast rations had been distributed and each soldier had performed his morning ablutions, the bugle sounded and each man fell into a column of march and moved out. It seemed to have been a very short march before they were halted along the outskirts of a huge Yankee encampment sprawling over thirty or so acres of a once manicured pecan orchard. The column was met by a small escort of Yankee officers who arrived with a Confederate major in tow. They were then marched into a small field bordering the Yankee camp and formed into lines at parade rest. The Yankee officers held back a short ways as the Confederate major rode forward and from horseback proceeded to brief the troops as best he could on what was expected of them. Carter listened carefully as the major relayed the terms of surrender which had been mutually agreed upon days earlier by generals Grant and Lee. As he finished his recitation of the surrender agreement, the major reminded each man that they were still representatives of the Confederacy and to act with honor throughout the process of disarmament, for as an army they had been defeated, but as the remaining members of a once beautiful way of life, they should submit without incident and therefore retain as much dignity as they might muster.

The disarmament passed quickly an without incident with the biggest surprise of the day being that each man was supplied with a hot meal once his weapons were turned in and each was given rations for three days travel. The commanding officer of the Yankee camp signed and presented a letter of passage to each soldier to make it known to any union patrols they encountered that they already had submitted and were free to travel. Many of Carter's fellow soldiers began to make camp near the Yankee's and talk circulated that a group was forming to head west and return fighting, but Carter wanted no such part of that. He said what few good-byes he wished and started homeward.

He had been marching for so long that his walk still carried the cadence and he covered much ground. He was used to living with hunger so he had stretched his Yankee rations to last him a week and now in his fifth day of homeward travel Carter was growing exhausted. The day-long hikes over the dry dusty roads which sprawled beneath that hot Georgia sun began to take their toll. Stopping by a low bridge, over top of a bubbling creek, he took a rest and ate one of his last cold biscuits. He ate slowly and filled his canteen in the creek and thought of the sights that had filled his eyes since leaving that Yankee camp. He'd seen plenty, the destruction and horror found on a battlefield and had well known the carnage that had lain in Sherman's wake as he pushed to the ocean. He had lived in rags, slept in mud and went hungry for quite a long time now, but this was worse. Now he faced first hand what had been shielded from him as a member of a military unit. Now he witnessed first hand the homelessness, pain and hunger that completely ravaged the families of the South. Everywhere he passed women, children, crippled and maimed soldiers, and freed slaves. All wandering, looking for family members. Looking for help. The half starved faces all wore the same look of hopelessness and hardship.

That night Carter spent camped beneath the outspread limbs of a giant live oak and was joined by a pair of homeless families seeking shelter beneath his tree. They were two young mothers and six small children, the oldest around ten. They had been made homeless and fatherless by the war and the women were so underfed that the skin appeared to hang from their once attractive faces. The children, some half naked, wore swollen bellies as testimony to their hunger and each had that same look about them of hopelessness. The young mothers invited him to share their supper as they made ready a cook fire and began to boil a pitifully thin soup consisting of a little salt, some wild onions and a mockingbird one of the youngsters had managed to catch that afternoon. Carter immediately offered to share what little he had left of his own larder, which the little families gratefully accepted and added to the pot.

II

Carter saw all too grimly that the destruction he'd seen along his way home had not been spared to the families in the southern parts of his home state and he tried to prepare himself for what he may find upon his return home. He tried to reassure himself that no matter what fate befell the little farm, they would be able to start over and rebuild as might be necessary. The fact that he would be among his family again was all that mattered and those thoughts of brother Seth and the old folks sped him along the last few miles until at last he trod upon familiar ground. As he turned up the dusty trail passing between a pair of overgrown and neglected fields, he barely recognized the ramshackle old building at the end of the lane which used to be home. He tried to ignore the burned out structure where the barn once stood, its charred beams standing ugly against the setting sun. He did give notice to a few shacks in the distance behind the house, surrounded by several Negroes milling about a couple of cook fires.

Upon reaching the front porch of the old home place, the door swung wide and out limped brother Seth sporting a wide grin and embraced him in a hug.

"By the grace of God ol' boy, you made it home!" His brother greeted him. "I prayed hard for you every day. Ma and Pa did too. They'd be mighty relieved to know your all right."

"I'm glad to see you too. It's good to see your up and around. Where's Ma and Pa?"

A coldness wrapped itself around his heart as he saw the change that came over his brothers thin face and he knew before Seth even spoke. His brothers sad eyes and furrowing brow, told him all he really needed to know.

"They're gone home for some time now Carter. I had no way of gettin' word out to you, not knowing where you'd be and all. I'm sorry you weren't here."

He just stared at his brother, not able to speak the question he most wanted to ask and his brother hugged him again. A few moments passed until Carter regained himself and choked out the question.

"How'd it happen Seth? What was it took them?"

"Several riders came to the farm wearing Reb uniforms, they demanded money and whiskey. Pa told them that he hadn't any of either but that they were welcome to stay for such victuals as was available. Turns out, they didn't want food, they were out looking for trouble."

Seth paused as Carter leaned back against a rail of the porch and gave him second to let it sink in before continuing.

"Some words were exchanged between Pa and the fellow who fancied himself as the groups leader in which it was revealed that they were deserters. Pa cussed them for being cowards and the man shot him in the stomach. Ma rushed out screaming for Pa and they shot her too. A few of them dismounted and tore through the house, but they didn't get much. Just some food stuffs and Pa's ol' pocket watch that Col. Tatum gave him for watching over the plantation when the colonel was down with a snakebite."

Carter remembered the watch. It was Pa's most valued possession. It had a picture of an owl etched on the front and a false back that popped open if you twisted it just right. It was in there that Pa kept a lock of Ma's blonde hair.

"Afterwards they just rode away as if nothing much had happened. Ma died right off. She was shot through the chest. Pa, he drug himself to where Ma was and held her till I come home." Seth had to stop for a bit as he teared up and motioned for Carter to join him on a split log bench which had adorned the old porch for many years. He had been taking it all in quite soberly and he took his seat and waited for his brother to continue.

"I had been over to the Creedmore property across the Flint river to see Mr. Creedmore's oldest daughter. Do you remember Lynne?"

Carter nodded.

"Well, that's what I found when I returned. Pa lived long enough to tell me the story, but he joined Ma during the night. When morning came, I went to report to the sheriff and to get the undertaker, but neither was available, so I went back to the Creedmore place again and they all turned out to help me tidy the bodies and do all that was necessary. Lynne read from the Bible and we sang some hymns. It weren't enough, but that's how I laid them to rest. I can take you to the graves in the morning Carter. It's getting dark now and you look like you can use a meal in you I expect. Come on in the house and we'll see what we can do about that."

Seth rose from his seat on the bench and led Carter inside. Once inside Carter caught the scent of cornbread baking and heard some rattling around in the kitchen.

"That's Lynne you hear in the kitchen. I asked her to marry me the day we laid the folks to rest. She's been awful good to this crippled old farmer." He rose his voice a bit toward the kitchen. "Lynne, come in here now, I've got a surprise for you!"

She came into the living room, wiping her hands on her apron. A lock of her red hair had fallen across her eyes and she pushed it aside as she looked up and recognized her brother in laws face. Tears welled up in her eyes and threatened to fall down her lightly freckled cheeks as she crossed the room to greet him. Carter hugged her shyly and greeted her with a smile.

"Oh Carter! I can't believe your home! We surely prayed for you."

"Thanks Lynne, and thanks for taking care of Seth and for the help you gave with my folks. I'm glad your here." He turned his eyes away and she could see he was a bit shocked from all the unexpected news.

"I see this is all pretty upsetting for you. Carter why don't you go on to your room? You'll find some fresh clothes and Seth will be along with some hot water for you to wash up in. I'll get back to supper and I'll see if you approve of my cooking. Okay?"

Carter did as suggested and during the evening meal Seth brought him up to speed on most of the news concerning the farm and their neighbors. They visited long into the night and not once did either brother mention his role in the war. Some things were best left unsaid.

He spent that night in the little room from his youth. It had only been a few years since he'd slept here, but the place was full of memories he couldn't now recall. He had found clothing, still packed neatly in his trunk, but the fit wasn't the same. He'd grown taller and thinner, barely making two hundred pounds. Stretching out on the old bed, he tried to organize his thoughts. In the last several hours, he'd had to absorb quite a lot. He wanted to cry for his folks, but couldn't. He wanted to hate himself for not having been there when they needed him, instead of following his brothers lead into the war, but knew it was silly to think that way. What had happened had happened and no amount of regret could change that now. He looked at the shadows in this little room and found no comfort in being there. He was woefully disassociated to the house. Everything had changed and the life he longed to return to was no more. Seth had married and would be wanting to start his own family and Carter felt that somehow he'd be in the way. Probably best to keep on the move he thought. He could always continue south, away from the war. Seth would hate to se him go, but Carter found no reason to stay now.

He lay thinking about before the war when Ma's brother had wired the family offering the two boys jobs on his ranch on the Caloosahatchee river down in Florida. He and Seth both suspected that Ma had written him and asked for the invitations in order to keep the boys from going to war. Carter had never met his uncle, Jefferson Davis Floydd, and considered taking the job, but when Seth returned from the army all shot up, well he felt duty bound to take his place and so never taken advantage of the opportunity. Perhaps, he should drift that way and look into the possibility of getting hired on now. Even if Uncle Floydd couldn't use him now, perhaps there would be other work enough to keep him from starving. Before he finally did find sleep, his mind was made up, he was going to Florida.

Carter's sleep had been dreamless and deep and as he awakened he noticed sunlight streaming in through the window. Obviously Seth had decided to let him sleep in, but how late it was he had no idea. He rose from the lumpy old mattress and dressed quickly. Looking forward to spending more time with his brother and new sister in law. The main room of the house was empty, but he could hear Lynne moving about in the kitchen, so he went over and sticking his head through the door found her fixing up some breakfast out of whatever she had on hand.

"Good morning." He said.

"Good morning to you," she replied, "did you sleep well last night?"

"I suppose so. But sleeping in a bed is gonna take some getting used too again."

"Well how's your appetite this morning? I'm afraid that I haven't any eggs or biscuits, but I've a pot of hominy on the stove and some warmed over rabbit from last night for you. I hope you'll enjoy it." She said with a smile and with an amusing tone added. "If I didn't know better Carter, I'd swear your folks had born twins. That blonde hair, blue eyes, and broad shoulders. I guess I'm a real lucky gal to marry into a family of such handsome men."

"Well, thanks. But Seth was always the pretty one. I guess that's how come he came to be married to the prettiest girl in South Georgia. And a awfully fine cook too. I didn't mention it last night, but supper was a pleasure and breakfast looks to be just as enjoyable."

"Good, I was hoping you'd be hungry this morning." She said as she set about preparing Carter a spot at the table.

"Where's my brother this morning?" He asked before being seated at his Ma's old oak table.

"He's done ate his share this morning. He said to apologize for his not waiting, but he had to get the workers organized this morning."

"What workers would those be? Do you mean the slaves I seen out back?"

"Yep, except they aint slaves anymore. They're all freed men and they came to settle back there in exchange for their labors. They've really been a blessing. This morning Seth's sending them over to Mr. Felt's place to raise his barn. The Yankees burned it out, same's ours. In exchange, next week Mr. Felt will send over wood from his saw mill and Seth can set them about rebuilding our own. Then he plans on taking back those two hay field out front from the weeds. They've been a lot of help." She set his plate before him and continued. "I reckon Seth'll be back in before too long. He won't be joining them this morning. He'd rather spend more time with you. I bet you've got plenty to talk about yet."

"I suppose we do at that. Lynne, how's his wounds. I see the limp, but how is he really?" Carter asked with care.

"He hurts Carter, sometimes I wonder how he gets out of bed each day, but he does. I rub him down often enough with liniment to ease his muscles, but he says that once he's up and around he loosens up and somehow he gets through the day. He hasn't much choice really, but I never hear him complain. Now if you will excuse me, I'll go get them dishes done." She left Carter to his morning meal and he wolfed it down and went out to find his brother.

Seth was just reaching the porch as Carter stepped out into the bright morning sunlight. Far out along the trail in, Carter could see the dust lifting as the negro workers made their way toward their distant neighbors farm.

"Good morning Carter, How'd you rest?"

"Fine, I guess it was more comfortable than sleeping in the mud after a long march."

"Yeah, I know all about that." Seth agreed. "Say, did you get some breakfast?"

"I just finished, thanks. You know that gal of yours is right handy in the kitchen. She's a fine woman Seth. I'm happy for you."

"Thanks."

The brothers grew quiet for a moment until Seth gently spoke and answered the very question Carter was having trouble getting around to asking.

"Ma and Pa's graves are over on the creek by the grove of peach trees Pa planted when we moved out here in forty-seven. They're on the backside of the grove nearest the creek and facing East. I'll walk out there with you if you'd like?"

"No, I'd like to talk some thing over with them. Thanks though, I'll be back up after awhile and we can catch up some more." Carter gave his brother a light smile and patted his shoulder as he descended the steps from the porch and headed out toward the creek to visit his folks at rest.

Sitting in the grass before the hand carved markers bearing the names of his parents, Carter looked over the sight Seth had chosen and felt that his brother had indeed chosen a fine place. The sound of the peach tree leaves fluttering in the light breeze combined with the gentle gurgling of the shallow creek water passing over the rounded stones, gave the place a quieting, calming, comfortable feel. The morning sun warmed his back as the blue sky spread above him and Carter allowed his focus to linger on the soft green of the grass upon which he sat, he watched the slow progress of an ant going about some journey of significance known only to itself. He sat for a long while before the markers, not thinking, just looking about and taking in everything around him until he finally found the strength to acknowledge the markers themselves. They had been simply constructed, neatly carved and made of resin pine. The smooth faces of each marker bore a Christian cross and the names of those who had borne him, raised him, fed, loved, and cared for him. He sat numbly for awhile before the not yet weathered markers and eventually Carter found his tears.

It started as a trickle down the cheek, but eventually he opened up and was overcome with great racking sobs of anguish, pain and loss. He cried not only for his folks, but for all those he'd badly wanted to grieve, but for so long now had been unable. He lay back in the sweet grasses and wept on, offering prayers to God to let his parents know how much he'd loved them.

Seth came from the orchard by early afternoon and found his brother red eyed and weary looking. He joined him in the grass and they sat together for a long time in silence. When Carter did speak, it was in a low almost apologetic tone.

"I'll be leaving soon Seth." He looked up into the startled eyes of his brother and continued. "Your the oldest, so I figure the farms rightfully yours. You've taken a wife now and you should be getting started on a family. Now that the folks are gone, I don't have much reason to stay. Your a good farmer and you've plenty of help, so I think it'd be best if I keep moving on."

"You can't be serious!" His brother cried out in disbelief. "Carter, your just now come home, sure things are different, but it can still be a good life here. This farm is half yours and I really hope you'll change your mind and stay. There's plenty of work to go around, I'll need you."

"No." Carter replied offering his brother a confident smile. "I can see you'll do just fine without me. I learned one thing well in the army and that was to march, to move along to new places and that's what I'll do. Staying here just doesn't feel right to me somehow."

With that said, Carter rose to his feet and offered his brother a hand in rising. Once Seth was on his feet and steady, Carter rested his hand on his brothers shoulder as they started back toward the house.

"I hope you won't think ill toward me? I rather hoped you would understand." Carter asked of his big brother.

"You must have given some thought as to where you'll be going then? I hear talk all of the time about opportunities with the railroad heading out West. In fact Lynne's cousin Charles left a couple of months ago to survey the routes. Perhaps we could send him a letter, he might be able to put in a word for you."

"Thanks, but nothing out west holds much appeal for me. Seth, do you remember when Ma's brother, uncle Floydd sent that letter offering us jobs on his ranch down in Florida? I was thinking of heading down that way. That states bound to bustin' out with growth from all the money the cattlemen made supplying the army with beef. Heck, I may find work that suits me long before I make it all the way down to the Caloosahatchee river country, but I think that's the direction

I'll be heading in. I remember some of his letters to Ma about trading with the Indians and trapping wild cattle in the brush. She said he had a sizable spread built up, I guess I'll go find out."

"Surely he won't deny kin a job." Seth said. "But, always know, your home will be waiting for you here if you ever find your way back to it."

III

The late Summer day was beginning to cool off as the sun made it's way lower toward the western horizon and the old gentleman sat working in the shade of the stables east wall. Seated upon an empty nail keg, he rested his back against the weathered old planks of the building while he worked a punch awl into the stirrup leather of an old saddle which had been long in need of repair. JD found himself able to catch up on more of the smaller repair jobs and chores around the ranch which always seem to get neglected throughout the year, since the doctor told him he must rest easy for awhile. Now, resting easy, he found no end of these little jobs to keep him quite busy. He was sure the doctor wouldn't approve, but at least he wasn't out in the saddle gathering a herd or out in the pasture clearing palmetto root, this was as idle as he was likely to get. There wasn't much on the ranch that was going undone though. Above all of his busy work he'd assigned to himself, there was more pressing business that needed attention. His riders had just completed a small roundup and culling out the yearlings and breeding stock, gathered a small herd for a drive West to the fort.

He paused in his chore and listened to the far away bawling of the cattle and swore under his breath. He wanted badly to join his riders and survey the gathering, but he had confidence in his crew. Especially the girl. He smiled about her. He always said she was twice the cowboy than most cowboys he'd hired drifting up and down the river at springtime roundup.

Just as he was returning to his chore the dinner bell began to ring. He smiled wide then as he heard his wife of thirty-eight years calling him to supper. He gathered his work and began putting each item away in it's place. He wasn't in a hurry, because he knew Luanne always rang the bell a bit early, to allow time for the hands to get in from the pastures and clean up before the meal. He carried the old saddle back into the back of the tack shed and set it up upon a rail that had been mounted along the wall for that purpose. He heard the riders approaching the corral and stepped out to the open doorway of the stable to watch them arrive. Pausing in the doorway he took in the view with approval. He enjoyed the harmony on the ranch and was proud of the place. 'The Big Cypress Cattle Company' he'd named it and he and Luanne had built this place on the banks of the Caloosahatchee River out of nothing more than a lot of blood, sweat, and determination and it did him good to think of how far they had come since settling here.

He had been young once and full of grit, but that was long ago. The grit was still there all right, but the youth had long ago faded. He moved out here with his pretty young bride, all set to tame the wilderness and raise a passle of kids. Some sons maybe, to help run things, but that wasn't meant to be. Sure they had the girl, Josephine, but she hadn't been born to them although they loved her as if she had. He smiled at her as she swung her horse into the compound and trotted over toward the stable where he stood.

"How's that herd coming along gal? Do you think they'll be fine for the night?" He asked her.

"They seem to be content holding right where they are. Henry and Charlie will nighthawk them and I'll send supper out to them. They figure to start herding them over to the fort first thing in the morning if that's all right with you." She said.

"That's just fine. I'll be glad to get them beeves sold and get that Yankee tax officer off of my back. I can't help but think I should go along, but those two'll get it done right. Heck, they've been herding for me since they were kids. I just hope they don't have any trouble, that's all." He worried out loud.

"They'll be fine." She said as she swung from her saddle and joined him on the ground. "They don't need a baby sitter and you certainly don't need to be in that saddle yet. Your health is a lot more important to us than a bunch of cows. I don't have to tell you, you really gave us all a scare there for awhile. So, don't go getting stubborn about it or I'll go tell Momma Luanne! Now you don't want her after you, do you?"

He feigned fright at her threat and they had a small laugh and she gave him a quick hug before walking her horse in to put him up for the night. She was right, the boys would be fine of course and he didn't need to worry her or Luanne. The doctor had said the problem was his heart, although the pain had been mostly in his left arm. He couldn't understand the doctors reasoning, but was in no position to argue with him. That was two weeks ago though and now he felt entirely better.

It all started one afternoon while he and a couple of his Indian cowboys were rebuilding the roundup corral out on the flats. He'd been real hot that day and found himself having a hard time catching his breath. Suddenly some white hot pains were shooting up his arm and he wasn't sure if he'd been snake-bit or lightning struck, but he knew something bad was going on for sure. Danny, one of the Indians helped him onto a horse and led him back to the house while another raced to the fort for the doctor who arrived the next day around noon.

Luanne and Josephine had sat up with him all through that evening and night wiping his forehead with cool cloths and keeping him as comfortable as they could. By the time the doctor arrived, JD was feeling much better, but consented to an examination anyway. That's when the doctor said his heart wasn't well and gave him some powders to take if he ever felt it starting up again. Then instructed him to stay away from any labor and out of the saddle for at least a month to give his heart some rest.

Josephine stepped from the building and took his hand as they walked up toward the house together.

"If your still worried, why don't you let me ride to the fort with them, I wouldn't mind at all?" She offered sweetly.

"No, the boys'll be just fine. Don't you mind me none gal. I just haven't been too at ease since that Yankee started coming around with that tax dun. But, once the boys are back, that'll be behind us and everything will be back to normal again. You'll see." He reassured her and squeezed her hand a little tighter.

IV

It wasn't much of an office, but it was all the good captain of the sprawling Fort Meyers, was able to provide to the assessors and surveyors office of the federal bureau of land taxes. The building hadn't seen a coat of paint in a good many years and the whole structure seemed to tilt inexplicably to the rear, giving visitors the feeling of walking down hill after having entered the office of Buford T. Fetterman, a smallish built, dark haired man whom bore the title of land agent and tax collector for the United States government. Inside the ten by fifteen foot office and seated about a makeshift desk, littered by all manner of plat and topographical maps, and across from Mr. Fetterman were Messrs. Alford Kennedy, a large, red-faced pig of a man and his associateWilliam Clinton, a tall weasel looking gent, newly arrived from Boston. They were gathered together over a rather heated conversation concerning a few thousand acres of improved bottom land up river from the fort.

"Buford, you promised us that dumb cracker would be folded under by now. You told us that there was no way he would be able to afford those back taxes and now your trying to tell me that he's paid them?" Kennedy was demanding to know.

"We received your letter and came at once on your word. On your word we've begun making plans to prep that land for cane farming and have contracted the initial seed stock from Havana. Now, you can sit there and tell us that we may not have the property. We moved on this and have the ball rolling because of you, therefore it's up to you to fix this Buford!"

"Please excuse Alford's short temper now Buford. Understand that he's upset about our sacrificing our investment and damaging our business reputation with our associates. What is our plan of action now, where do we go from here?" Clinton offered in a less excited manner.

"Look fella's," Buford began. "it's not over yet. How was I supposed to know the Reb's had payed that old geezer in gold all those years? Sure he was able to make the note on his back taxes, but I happen to know it took everything he had. So I did a bit of adjusting to his account and it seems there's still a matter of some late charges accumulated in the amount of six hundred dollars. I served the papers myself on him and he told me he hadn't the money to cover it. You see boys, thirty days from the date he was served, I can double that tax debt. Sixty days passes and I can double it again. Ninety days passes and I post a notice to sell that property at the gates of this fort and all you have to do is step in with the money. The selling price will still be about what you figured to get it for anyway. You just have to wait a couple of more months, that's all."

"You'd better be straight with us on this Buford. You stand to lose as much as us if this deal goes bust." Kennedy chimed in again with his almost threatening tone.

"How can you be so confident he can't come up with the money? He's surprised you before." Clinton asked.

"Like I said, I served these papers to him myself. He told me that the only way to cover this debt was to gather a herd and bring them in to sell here at the fort or out at the stockyards by the docks. But remember, even if he raises a herd, he has to get those cows delivered here right? He won't be using barges to bring that many head down river, so he'll be driving them in. There's only one trail between here and the B3C ranch. It may cost you both a couple of dollars, but there are always enough drifters down at the docks that would be willing to help you see to it that herd never reaches this fort." Buford suggested matter of factly.

"How many cows will he have to raise to cover that note?" Kennedy asked a little calmer.

"Forty or so at today's market price. But, I expect him to bring along a few more than he'd need, just to be safe." Buford told them.

"Forty? That shouldn't be too hard for him to raise. Do you think he'll have a buyer?" Kennedy asked with concern.

"Gentlemen, if that herd gets through, he'll have a buyer. You can bet on it. That's why you two need to see to it that they don't make it." Buford explained.

"We understand." Clinton said with a hard look toward Kennedy. "We'll take care of it. You just keep up your end here. We don't want anymore surprises, right?"

"No, we don't. Now gentlemen, if you'll excuse me, I really must be getting back to work." That said, Buford arose from his chair and shook hands with his two conspirators, each in turn.

Once outside the office, Alford Kennedy and William Clinton crossed the square compound of the fort and headed out the main gate along the road leading toward the long rows of buildings and docks lining the waterfront. As they walked they continued to work over the news Fetterman had given them and what it might mean to their venture.

"Alford, I must be on the sloop heading to St. Augustine tomorrow evening, so I don't have to tell you that this is in your hands and I'm counting on you to keep things on track." Clinton was saying.

"You don't have to remind me of your schedule William. I'm having a hard time trusting that Fetterman right now. If he's wrong, we're through. Do you understand my concerns?" Kennedy asked gravely.

"I do. But, all the same, you'd best do as he suggests and gather a few hard cases to watch that trail in. To my way of thinking, the sooner the better. I have no idea when that old fool will be trying to bring in those cows, but we'd better have someone in place to stop him. Just, be sure to tell them not to kill him. Losing a few head of cows is one thing, but if they leave a body or two out in the palmettos, there'll be full investigation and I don't want that kind of attention. Got it?"

"So what of the cows, you don't want me to have them shot do you? What should they do with them?"

"Alford I don't give a hoot what they do with them, let the hired boy's have them to sweeten the pot, just be sure they're never sold around here. Have them drive them to Punta Gorda or Tampa or someplace, but never let them be seen around Fort Meyers."

They stopped walking and in a lower tone Clinton added this.

"Look Alford, I've arranged to have an additional hundred thousand dollars worth of investment shares to be sold in Boston and France. I'll be meeting this Dabria fellow next week in St. Augustine and from his correspondence, I'm certain, he'll account for a good number of those shares. Just stay away from Buford, but keep a weather eye out on the deal. When I return this mess with the cows should be over and we'll be able to follow this thing through. I'm going back to my room now to pack. I'll see you in the morning."

Then turning away each man continued on toward his own way.

V

By the time Carter had made his way into Florida, Autumn had begun to bring a chill to the morning breeze. A front had moved over, leaving puddles all along the roadways near the docks of the St. Johns river. Travelers from all over huddled together wrapped in coats and shawls, some complaining bitterly about the unseasonable weather as they awaited the arrival of the big, side wheel paddle steamer which would take them upriver to the south. This town of Jacksonville seemed enormous to Carter. It was filled with all manner of buildings and businesses, but Carter had hoped to find work on a vessel heading upriver in return for passage. He wandered the marina, passing amongst the gatherings of travelers until spying a heavily loaded barge being positioned at the docks for unloading and made his way to the mooring and offered his labors to a short, stocky man with wide set eyes and a squarish jaw whom greeted Carter with an Irish lilt.

"By the look of you, there's likely something on yer mind. Well, out with it son, we've got work to attend to." The man offered.

"Carter, call me Carter. As you may have guessed, I need a job. I'm looking to head upriver and hope to trade work for the ride. I've got a good strong back and I can work alongside of any man all day."

"It's a good proposition Lad. However, I'm not the man to do the hiring," He said good naturedly, "I only work on this barge for Colonel Hart. We haul fruit down river from Palatka and back here to Jacksonville. We always seem to be needing new men on the return trip upriver, so you go see about the job with a man named Jason Partridge. He's the warehouse foreman and distributor of the Colonel's citrus. You see all these crates lad? They're full of tangerines. Each crate holds four bushels and I've got here nearly ninety crates. We've delivered seven loads such as this already this season and will be making this trip a good many more times delivering grapefruit and oranges. Come springtime when the shipping is over, the Colonel will usually offer employment in the groves themselves. There's always plenty of work about the plantation that's for sure. Now, you'd best be heading over to the warehouse yonder and seeing Mr. Partridge about that job. If he takes a shine to you, you can be back in time to help unload all this citrus. In fact, I've done all the talking, but already, I like you. You tell him I said so. My names Collin O'Hara, but me friends all call me Bull. Run along lad. I've work to do, but don't worry. There'll be plenty more when you return."

Carter hurried toward the rows of warehouses and entered the one Bull had indicated. A team of draft horses pulled an enormous cart with the lettering 'HART'S GROVES, EST. 1856' through the doors of the warehouse bound for the loading dock as he approached the building in search of the foreman. Once inside, he introduced himself to a tall thin fellow wearing a black bowler hat and smoking a hand rolled cigar.

"My names Carter Holder. I'm looking for Mr. Jason Partridge. Would he be about?"

"Good morning Mr. Holder. What is it you want with Partridge?" The fellow asked around his cigar?

"I was sent from the dock by Collin O'Hara. He said for me to ask Mr. Partridge about a job on the Colonels barges. Are you Mr. Partridge?" Carter asked.

"Quite right. Come with me and we'll see about it. My office is right over here." He said, finally removing the cigar and leading Carter into a small room littered with all manor of books, ledgers, and shipping schedules.

Clearing off a seat in front of his small wooden desk, he invited Carter to be seated, then positioned himself across from him and began to dig through a drawer for a pencil, then looking up asked him directly.

"You running from something boy?"

"No!" Carter said defensively. "For a fact, I'm not running from anything. I'm just hoping to work enough to pay for a passage upriver. I just feel the need to travel, that's all."

"Sure, that's how I had it figured. I see a lot of men passing upriver these days. Most not knowing where their going, but still itching to get there. That you boy? You drifting or do you have a destination in mind?"

"I have a destination, but I'm not expected. How about it? Do I get the job?" Carter asked a bit uncomfortable with the questioning.

"Sure, I'll make you the same deal I make every drifter looking to work his way upriver. You see everybody wants to Pole the empty barges South, but no one wants to bring them back down river, even though you travel the loaded barge with the current. So, what I propose is for you to make three trips upriver and back for which I'll offer you three dollars a trip, plus meals." He paused and re-lit his cigar.

"It takes five days to make it upriver to Palatka from here with an unloaded barge. A day is spent loading on the docks and your four days back down river to here fully loaded. Remember the loaded barges will be riding the current. You make those three trips upriver and I'll pay you your wages when you return. Then, your back upriver on a barge with nine dollars in your pocket and no obligation to return. Does that sound fair Carter?"

"It does. Shall return to the dock then?" Carter asked with a smile.

"Give me your hand and word as a gentleman, and we have a deal." He said rising.

Carter did give his word and shook on the arrangements, then hurried back to report to Bull.

"Get yerself a job, eh lad?" Bull asked with mock surprise.

"Yes sir Mr. O'Hare, where do I start?" Carter asked.

"Well first thing, it's Bull. I done told ya me friends all call me Bull and I hope yer to be my friend lad or this will be a long trip upriver."

"Very well Bull, put me to work." Carter responded with good humor.

Carter unloaded crates of fruit from the barge then loaded them upon the wagon he'd seen brought up earlier. When it was full, the team was led back into the warehouse where it was unloaded as Carter and his crew mates were allowed a rest. At the end of the afternoon, Carter's muscles were aching as he helped load the last crate aboard the wagon. He retrieved his personal gear from the warehouse where he'd left it for the day and stowed it on board the barge. There were two other crew member other than Bull aboard the barge, but for the most part, they kept to themselves. Their lack of conversation was not missed however, for Bull kept up enough talk for them all and when he wasn't talking he'd be whistling an Irish jig as he worked and Carter liked this man immediately.

That evening as the work was completed and night was quickly gathering, Bull approached the barge carrying a cloth sack which contained several bottles of bourbon; one of which he offered to share with Carter as they rested upon the barge and told Carter of the company and the rules of employment.

"Rule number one on this ship, my lad, is no drinking." Bull said quite seriously.

"What are we doing now Bull?" Carter said with amusement.

"Shhh lad. I'm Irish. For an Irish man, there are exceptions." He explained.

"Well, I'm not Irish."

"Perhaps not lad, but your drinking with an Irishman and that'll count close enough, now stop interrupting. Rule number two is that there's to be no fighting on board. Just follow the Good Book's advise and turn the other cheek, for I'll not tolerate it. If you absolutely cannot get along with a crew mate, I'll beach the barge and set you afoot at the nearest opportunity of my convenience. Do you understand that Lad?"

Carter nodded affirm as he prepared to take a pull from the bottle Bull had just offered him.

"Good." Said Bull, "I figured you for an even temper already. Now the third rule of conduct involves topics of conversation. I'll prefer that there be no mentioning of the war, any related politics, preference of religion or red headed women."

"That doesn't sound too unreasonable, but may I ask why?" Carter asked while trying to mask his amusement.

"Because any conversing on the war, politics and religion inevitably leads to disagreements which can lead to fights. Now I refer you to rule number two. As for red headed women, I've never met one that didn't break my heart or steal me blind, although I did marry one once."

"And did she break your heart too Bull?" Carter asked, enjoying his companion.

"No, she didn't just break it. She ripped the poor bustard out and stomped it flat she did. It rightly weren't her fault alone, but I'll never chance that again I wager. So rather than lead me into temptation with talk of the volatile vixens, I'd much prefer to avoid the subject altogether."

Carter took another sip from the bottle and passed it back to Bull who up ended it for a couple of deep gulps.

"How often do you find yourself breaking rule number one Bull?"

"I told you lad, the rules don't apply to me. I can't be breaking a rule if the rule doesn't apply to me, so I take a drink every now and then to keep me humble. You see, God made whiskey to keep the Irish from ruling the world and since I seek neither fortune nor fame, I shall live up to divine providence and maintain my humility."

"Tell me about the barge Bull. We cast off in the morning and I don't know my job yet. What is it you'll have me doing?" Carter asked his humble friend.

"Son, your to be a poleman on this here barge while we're afloat. We'll be working in teams of two with a team on each side of the barge. You will be teamed with me. We start out at the front of the side walk on the barge and get a good set with your pole, then walk and push your way back, you'll find the days pass quickly once you've established a routine. It's forty-four steps from one end to the other and by the time we reach Palatka, you'll know those steps well. Lunch will be taken about noon of the day and we pole the remainder of the time. The work is not hard lad, if you put your back into it. If you try to push all day with your arms, you'll wear down quickly. The trip south is by far the worst of the runs. Although the boat will be empty, we'll be facing the current the entire trip. You see, this river is different than any other I've been on. It runs a contrary course from South to North the whole way. The Indians called it 'Il-La-Ka' which means 'river that wanders against itself'." Bull paused for a pull on the bottle before continuing on.

"Night time comes and we'll tie up out of the channel with lanterns hung to keep a larger vessel from running us over. Even during the daytime we have to be vigilant of the steamers and such. The larger vessel always gets the right of way, so it's our job to be on watch at all times."

"What of the other two? What can you tell me about them?" Carter asked curiously.

"Not much I'm afraid." Bull told him between sips. "I've known them a short while and they are rather quiet men that keep to themselves. We get along well enough and I expect you'll have no quarrels. They made the same bargain with Mr. Partridge as yourself and they've just completed their first run upriver and back. Now, get yourself between a few of them empty crates and drape your tarp over you, it'll at least keep the dew off while you rest and rest as much as you can. I'll be needing you fresh for the morning. Good night!" Bull finished with a flurry and hopped up from the crate he'd been seated on and headed off a bit to bed himself down for the night.

Morning broke with a cool and crisp with a heavy dew glittering in the rising sunlight. Steam rose from the water and fog pooled into banks without a breeze to disperse it, and obscured much of the sights of the city as the barge left anchorage and began it's crawl upriver. The sun had yet to rise above the horizon when Bull had awakened Carter for the days work and as he walked his push pole along the barge's walk way he watched the river bank slide past. In breaks within the forest, up from the waters edge, he spied groups of travelers standing around large fires to help break the morning chill and couldn't help himself, but to chuckle to himself remembering his fathers lesson about building a warming fire.

"Wise men build a small fire. They can get up real close and stay warm. But, a fool always builds a big fire. Then he has to stand way back and he's still cold." He used to say.

By mid morning, Jacksonville had been left far behind, but the river still teemed with traffic of all sorts. Canoes, rafts, and Jon boats were being paddled on their way. Undoubtedly loaded with furs, feathers and other trade goods. Whole families at times would row past, off to find a new start, same as himself and Carter offered a prayer beneath his breath that each would find it. Often the passed tall masted schooner, federal patrol boats and the large steamers with the side mounted paddle wheels. Carter regularly waved at the passenger of the grand steamers, a bit jealous over how comfortable they allowed themselves to travel. Poling a barge, however, was quickly proving to be a much more enjoyable way to travel, than by advancing in a column of march. Carter wondered if he may have missed a great opportunity by not enrolling in the navy. It was many miles of poling until they reached the point where the rivers channel narrowed. At this point the larger vessel traffic seemed to thin out a good bit. They were now passing far enough South that signs of man encroachment upon the land was nowhere evident. For miles on end the were passing great stands of bald cypress and hammocks of live oak, all interspersed with and surrounded by maple, bay, cabbage palm, willow, pine and the stately magnolia. He noticed a few fruit trees mixed into the hardwoods at interesting intervals. He spied wild orange, persimmon, grape and banana, whose broad leaves were yellowing in the early cold.

Carter was excited about the wild, tropical beauty of the forests he poled by. Green was still the color of the landscape here and would remain so year round due to the short lived Winter months.

Wildlife abounded here as well. Carter regularly saw deer , bear, bobcat, fox and hundreds of species of birds along the waters edge. Many turtles were showing themselves as the day warmed and pulled themselves from the water to lay upon logs protruding from the water at places along the channels edge. The creature which most captured Carter's attention was the alligator. Just like the turtles, they were sunning along the rivers edge as the day warmed and there was a good many to see. Their sizes all ranged less than three foot long which Bull explained was due to the heavy prices being offered for the hides. This was still a busy stretch of river and the adult gator's had long ago succumbed to mans need for a handsome pair of boots.

Nearing the noon hour, Bull called the break and the four polemen set about anchoring the craft in place so the current didn't reclaim any of their progress while they ate. One of the other men on board, whose names he'd recently learned were Leon and Billy, built a small fire in an iron pot which had been attached to the fore deck and intended for that purpose. Once it was kindled and burning, Bull prepared some salt cured ham and cold biscuits to be eaten for lunch. Coffee was soon boiling to wash down the lunch and no sooner had the last biscuit disappeared and the last drop of coffee downed. The anchors were pulled and they resumed the steady pace of poling against the current.

Throughout the afternoon, Carter and Bull would call out back and forth to each other with ribbing and good natured jokes. More than once Carter would send out a joke to one of the other two crew mates, but neither seemed inclined to join in the playful conversation.

Once night fell over the river, they pushed themselves well out of the middle of the channel and anchored fast. Lanterns were hung about and supper was prepared and consumed in the same manner as lunch. When the meal was over Leon and Billy excused themselves to the aft section of the barge and sat quietly talking. Carter was actually quite tired and looked forward to a bit of rest when Bull brought up the matter of his diplomatic immunity to the first rule of river travel and produced another bottle of bourbon. After a few belts to lubricate his tongue, Bull warmed up some of his best stories and entertained Carter long into the night.

The rest of the journey mirrored the first day and passed uneventful until the afternoon of the fifth day, when they puled up to a large hewn cypress landing along a wide stretch of river. A hand painted sign hung alongside the landing, welcoming travelers to 'HART'S GROVES, PALATKA'. After tying up to the landing Leon jumped to the dock and rang a large triangle bell like Ma used to call him in for supper. Minutes later, hoofbeats signaled the arrival of a large Negro riding a fine gray mare coming down the dark trail that lead into the forest as far as Carter could see.

"Ah thoughts that'd be ya'll comin' in Mista Bull. If'n ya'll wait jus' a bit, I'll let Massuh Hart know ya'll is ready to load up agin'. They'll be only a minute or so fo' the wagons get down here an ya'll be gettin' loaded up agin'. Ah'll be right back fo' ya know'd it suh!" With that he turned his horse and galloped away.

Soon wagons arrived with a crew of Negroes who helped to load the barge full of fruit for the return trip back down river. After the wagons had left and Bull was satisfied that everything was in order. He led Carter down the path from the landing, which led to the plantation headquarters. After an eighth of a mile hike through tropical wilderness, the trees began to thin and eventually gave way to well manicured groves of orange and other citrus trees. Several open fronted structures were located in the forward area of a great open plain which sprawled before him. These barn-like out buildings stored hundreds of crates for shipping the Colonels fruit and also housed a fair collection of farming tools and supplies.

A few lean too type shelters had been erected amongst several rustic looking shotgun houses which lined one end of an oak hammock in the not too far off distance. Cook fires had been kindled and a large bunch of Negroes were gathering for the evening meal beneath the outspread branches of the oaks. Across the way stood the main house. It was not quite as larger nor antebellum as the plantation houses Carter was accustomed to seeing, but looked quite comfortable and stately.

Evening flights of duck and heron filled the darkening sky as they winged overhead, crying their wild calls as they approached the house and knocked.

A kindly old gentleman invited them in saying that the Colonel would join them soon. There were others in the house awaiting the Colonel and introductions came quickly. Jim Aull the plantation overseer, Paul Badness the labor foreman, and Samuel Caphart the high sheriff of Palatka were milling about while enjoying cigars an brandy while waiting for the Colonel to join them. Soon the Colonel entered the room with his nurse and greeted his visitors warmly. Upon reaching for Carter's hand he seemed pleased to meet a new face and introduced himself.

"Colonel C. J. Hart is my name. Welcome to my home." He said with a slight bow.

"Carter Holder Sir," replied Carter, bowing himself. "I'm pleased to meet you Colonel Hart. I'm new in your employ. Mr. Partridge hired me in Jacksonville and Mr. O'Hara has been showing me the ropes."

"Tell me sir, from whence do you come? Your accent suggest a native son of Ol' Dixie, but what part?"

"Georgia Sir. Decatur county along the Flint river. I left home four years ago following General Longstreet and since the war is over, I haven't lost my taste for travel." Carter allowed.

"Carter," volunteered sheriff Caphart. "if your looking for a place to settle, you can do worse than settling here in Palatka. There's still plenty of prime land around here and the city is growing up. Lord knows there's plenty of work to go around, a fine opportunity to settle if you ask me."

"I'll consider that, but only after my employment obligations to the Colonel are met." Carter spoke consideringly.

As the Colonel greeted Bull fondly, Bull turned over a ledger to him .

"Here's the delivery count and purchase orders signed by Mr. Partridge. All went well on the run and we're set to be off again come first light. The boys have loaded a split cargo of navels and grapefruit. The weathers been in our favor and the currents been running smoothly. I don't expect we'll find any trouble back down river from here." Bull spoke proudly.

"Good news then." Said the Colonel. "I guess you and this young man had better go see Miss Lillie Mae in the kitchen and get you some supper. I'll have her fix your rations for the barge and they'll be delivered in the morning as usual. Good night Bull."

"Good night Sir." Bull replied while already leading Carter through the house and exited by way of the dining room leading out to a covered walkway which ran some forty or so feet up to a smaller building. The walkway was covered with split cypress shingles, but open on both sides except for handrails which reminded Carter of hitching posts. Along the sides of the walkway were rocking chairs.

Bull explained that this was the breezeway to the kitchen and that most proper cracker homes had one, for during the summer it could get too hot to cook in the house and if a fire ever started, the main house was easier to defend from the flames.

Upon reaching the door to the kitchen, Bull knocked twice and called out sweetly.

"Miss Lillie Mae, me darling lass. Yer Irish lover has returned again to ye. Is it in yer heart to receive me?"

No sooner had Bull finished than the door swept back and out stepped the tallest, widest, and blackest woman, Carter had ever seen. She stepped from the doorway, wiping her oversized hands on her well worn apron hem with a hard scowl.

"You cut out all 't love talk you carryin' on 'fore I wash dat mouth o' your'n out wit' me some good lye soap, 'cause eer'body knows that they aint no flickerin of a feelin' fer love in dat fool Irish heart. The onliest thing you might got dat has a feelin' in it is yo' gut. Now, aint I right?" She said scoldingly to Bull.

"Of course not dear," Bull says with a pained look on his face, "you know I look forward to seeing you every time I make it back for a night."

"Huh! All you lookin' forward to is my cookin', you ol' Devil. Who's at you got taggin' ya tonight?" She asked eyeing Carter.

"Carter Ma'am, I'm pleased to meet you and I haven't even tasted your cooking yet!" He said, stepping up with a grin.

Lillie Mae melted then and brought forth a wide smile full of big white teeth.

"Aint tasted my cookin' yet? Well get on in here boy, I can fix dat. Yall otha' ol' boys' done come and gone, but dey's plenty left fo' sho'. I knowed to be expectin' ya'll so I made plenty. Now come on." she turned aside and hustled them on past her.

"They's spare plates and such over there by dat wash basin. grab a plate and tell me what ya wants an' don' be shy, dey's plenty.

And plenty was right. she had sliced venison roast seasoned with wild onions and garlic, boiled potatoes, corn bread, fried catfish, fried turtle, sour dough biscuits, and swamp cabbage. She even had sour orange pudding for desert. Carter couldn't remember when he'd seen so much food and asked if it was a holiday he'd forgotten or if she cooked like this everyday.

"Food don' keep too well down here. the airs too moist. So, when I get somethin' to cook, I cook it. Ever' day I gets somethin' different on my stove, all depending on what I get to work with. One thang too, de colonel Hart, he belives in fillin' de mens bellies up. H knowed dat they gonna work a full day's work if'n they gets a full belly. And don' you know, I believe that ver' same thing." Said Lillie Mae as she piled their plates high.

Later that night aboard the barge, Carter lay awake amongst the crates, feeling full and lazy. The nights had warmed considerably and the night sky above him was coated with pale clusters of stars clear and bright. The second quarter moon rode high in the sky providing a gentle wash of light across the river. Frogs sang gently along the banks of the water course, mixing their nocturnal harmony with that of the grunting gators and the ever inquisitive barred owl. A soft scent of orange blossoms floated on the breeze and as Carter drifted off to a deep comfortable sleep.

The blue light of early dawn found the crew shaking off the nights comforts and preparing to shove off from the Colonels dock. Bull and Leon were working at the stern of the barge erecting a tripod with an oarlock, into which they fitted a long paddle to use as a rudder. The current would be propelling them downstream and Bull intended to use the paddle only to keep them from spinning in the current. Direction changes along the bends in the river would still be carried out with aid of the push poles, but Carter quickly learned that this was to be a very easy trip. during a particularly long stretch of river Carter took advantage of his first real opportunity to get to know his other two companions and joined Billy by the stem of the vessel sitting on crates.

"Will this be your last turn upriver on the barge?" Carter asked him.

"Yep, and I can't say I'll miss it all that much. I served for a time under JEB Stuart and I've come to know that if a man is supposed to travel, he ought to be mounted on a fine horse."

"I was in the war too. I was a private in Longstreet's brigade. I didn't know you served." Carter said.

"How could you have known? I never spoke of it. For a time I was Lieutenant William Pickford Starling. Now I'm just Billy again. I don't really like to talk of the war though and what's become of us all. Some memories are still too hard."

"True enough, I never dwell on it myself. I fought on foot myself. I marched with the infantry from South Georgia, all the way to Pennsylvania and back and I can tell you, floating down this river beats marching any day." Carter offered and brought a smile from the man.

"Where ya'll heading after we get back Billy?"

"Turpentine camps over in Ocala. It's hard work, but it does pay a decent wage. Leon's cousin owns a camp and it don't make no never mind to me, but if you want to join us later, he might could get a word in for you. Think it over some."

"Thanks, but I've other plan. I'll be heading farther South."

"Suit yourself, but whatever it is your heading too. Good luck." Billy then got up and walked back to take his turn at the paddle.

Time passed quickly on the river and before he knew it, Carter was on the third trip of his commitment to his employers and found himself again at the office of Jason Partridge.

"I wish you'd consent to stay on a while longer. Bull says your a good man and I need good men to get that fruit up here from Palatka. How about it Carter, give us a few more runs on the river and I'll give you a little something extra for staying. What say?" Partridge was asking around his ever present cigar.

"Thank you for the offer, but no. I've reason to be getting upriver some more and I plan to get as far South as I can by boat. Then I suppose I'll have to march on from there. You see, my uncle is a cattleman down on the Caloosahatchee river and I'm going to his place." Carter explained.

"Well then here's good news for you. My brother Ray runs the trading post on Lake George. He buys furs, plumes, and trade goods from the crackers that live farther South. If you make it to his place on Lake George, you might catch on with one of his traders who can guide you South through the narrows. Going to the Caloosahatchee, you can take St. Johns all the way south and then cross over into the Kissimmee river. That takes you through Okeechobee and into Caloosahatchee. Heck son, you can practically ride the whole way down in a good dugout. Just be sure to watch yourself in them wilderness stretches. With all the drifters coming into the state, you can never be too careful when you meet another soul. Between here and Lake George it aint bad because of the Yankee patrol boats, but farther South be on guard. I recommend partnering up with an experienced traveler, because Florida offers a few challenges that you might not have seen yet."

"Thanks for the tip, I'll go see him right off."

"You do and tell him I look forward to seeing him up this way real soon. Good bye Carter."

Carter spent the rest of that evening getting outfitted with the money he'd received from Partridge. He stopped in at a few of the storefronts that lined the streets near the waterfront and bought himself a couple loose fitting cotton shirts and a pair of canvas breeches made popular by that Strauss fellow out West. His army cap he figured to keep and his boots had plenty of sole left. They had been practically new when he'd taken them from a Yankee cavalry officer. They were high topped and low heeled and hadn't been much to march in, but it sure beat going barefoot.

After making his purchases he counted what money he had left and figured he better get himself a gun. There was no way to know what he'd run into down South and if he could hunt, at least he would eat well. Carter was directed to a shop nearby that was fully stocked in firearms of all shapes and sizes. He picked out a used Colt cattleman's rifle in .45 caliber along with a couple of boxes of cartridges. After haggling with the store owner a bit Carter walked out fully heeled and penniless.

The barge moved steadily upriver, slowly fighting the current. Bull and Carter had resumed their steady work pace across from two new polemen sent aboard by Mr. Partridge.

They had been underway for some time before Bull spoke his mind.

"You'll be missed by me lad. I've grown fond of your company. I know you've got yer uncle's place to be headin' to, but I wish you'd remain a bit longer with me here. Why, ye haven't yet heard all of my jokes and your the only one that'll laugh at them."

"Well Bull, why don't you come long with me. I'm gonna miss them jokes if we split up now and Mr. Partridge told me to get an experienced partner. Besides, aren't you overdue for a change anyway?" Carter asked, hoping he'd agree.

"I'll not lie to you. I've been thinking on that very same thing. I've more than done my time on this river, but stayed so long for a lack destination. I don't think the colonel will hold my leaving against me. If your serious, I think I will join you although I expect the traveling to be rough. My one reservation is that yer Uncle doesn't know me from Adam. It may be he's not any room for me."

"Well, we can cross that bridge when we get to it. It may turn out that he's been waiting for a high toned pair like us to show up, so he can make us all rich. It does give me more confidence knowing that you'll be along." Carter said, excited about the new turn of events.

VI

The three men sat beneath the shade of a stand of maple lining the cattle trail, which paralleled the Caloosahatchee river as it flowed to the gulf past Fort Meyers. The trees were brilliantly green this time of year and had begun sprouting new leaves for the early Spring which had begun to arrive and stood clustered behind a screen of low growing cabbage palms. This little grove of maple had been the men's campsite for the last three days, allowing them to remain hidden from the river and still offering them a fine view of the trail they expected to find cattle driven in on any day now. Their beds were not more than three depressions nestled into the soft earth beneath the shelter of the maples. They had been camping without benefit of a fire, lest the smoke or flame alert others to their presence. Their horses, which remained saddled most of the time, were picketed behind the maples in the protection of an elderberry thicket. Each night under cover of night fall, the horses were led to the river to drink and the saddles removed and each in turn given a good rub down. The many discomforts of a dry camp were only a minor burden to the men as they lounged there in the shade, each with a pair of shiny new ten dollar gold pieces in his pocket, with the promise of an additional twenty dollars apiece once their job was completed.

The job was to intercept a small herd of cattle being driven into the fort from the B3C ranch upriver. Once they had gained possession of the herd they had agreed to cross to the North side of the river and drive toward Punta Gorda and a secure market. Actually the man who'd hired them said he really didn't care what they did with them so long as they never reached Fort Meyers. They lay still among the shadows of the maples as a gentle afternoon breeze blew in, bringing with it the unmistakable popping sound of a whip being cracked.

Quickly the trio went into action as soon as they herd the noises. The horses were brought up and the saddles cinched tightly. Bed roles were folded neatly and packed away behind saddles. They quickly checked over the loads in the revolvers which were kept ready, holstered outside their pants and they mounted up and rode out to earn their pay.

Dust formed in low hanging clouds about the feet of the cattle as they made their way along the trail which followed the river. The morning air had been fairly cool with occasional breezes passing over them, swaying the treetops gently along the rivers edge. The two Indians were in no hurry and had so far let the cattle find their own pace as they made their way toward the fort. Mr. Floydd had asked them to drive this small herd to sell at the army fort and they were both very proud of the trust he placed in them. They rode to the rear of the shuffling herd, watching for stragglers and occasionally cracking the whip to keep them moving onward along the trail. The sky above showed a deep blue and the air was clean and fresh. Today was a good day for driving cattle.

Both drovers were Calusa Seminoles, but were dressed more like white cowboys than indians. The only visible giveaway to their ethnicity was the dark skinned faces peaking out from beneath the battered felt hats riding high upon their heads. Henry Osceola was the older of the two and therefore assumed the role of trail boss, although it was just the two of them. Charlie Jumper was his companion's name, both men having ridden together many times in Mr. Floydd's employ. They had come to work for the aging cattleman part-time, many years ago. They worked each roundup and most drives for him since they both were young boys. Now the cattleman was sick and they drove the herd for the first time without him.

The lead cows stopped and stared confused as three men rode from the brush directly in to their path. The two indians rode to the front of the herd together, to inquire what was going on.

"Why do you not let us pass? We are taking these cows to the fort for Mr. Floydd. Why do you stop our herd?" Henry asked, facing the three gunmen who sat stride their mounts holding drawn revolvers in their hands.

Ignoring Henry, the middle man spoke to his companions.

"Look at this boys. We just found ourselves a couple of rustlers."

"We're not rustlers Mister, I told you. We are driving these beeves to the fort for Mr. JD Floydd. That is his brand upon each of them." Henry said calmly, disguising the fear that was enveloping him.

"Boy?" The middle man acknowledged Henry for the first time. "Do ya'll know what we do to rustlers around here?"

"I am aware, but I tell you again, we do not rustle these cows. If you wish to follow us to Fort Meyers, there will be men there who know this brand and know that I speak honestly. Now, please let us pass."

The riders sat their mounts, gun drawn, and seeming to enjoy having the upper hand.

"You boys get off of them ponies before I decide to just shoot you right out of your saddles." The middle man spoke again and leveled his cocked pistol right at Henry's face.

Without further argument, the two indians dropped from their saddles and stood before the trio of gunmen. Charlie whispered something to Henry in Seminole and the outlaw closest to him rode forward and belted him across the forehead with the barrel of his gun. Henry watched horrified as his partner crumpled to the ground, a dark line of blood already beginning to run across his face. Charlie rolled over in the dirt and groaned. The man who'd hit him dismounted and walking over, Kicked the young Indian violently as he lay in the dust of the trail. Henry heard ribs breaking as the outlaw kicked his friend a couple of more times as he lay there. Henry stood motionless unable to help his friend.

The gunman that had done the talking up until now ordered the other two to tie both of the indians with their hands behind their backs. One of them pulled out a knife and cut the reins from Charlie's mount to tie them up with. Charlie was dragged back to his feet and stood coughing on unsteady legs as his hands were bound behind his back. Blood dripped from the cut on his forehead and mixed with the dirt from the trail, leaving him a ghastly sight.

"Boy, we're gonna teach ya'll a lesson you won't ever forget." The man spoke as he stepped up close to Henry and caught him full across the mouth with a wicked punch which cut both lips. He could taste blood in his mouth as the outlaw ripped into him with a savage two fisted attack that left him sprawled out in the dirt on his back. He looked to his right and could see Charlie being held up from behind as the other man punched him repeatedly in his face and stomach. He rolled over and pulled his knees up under him, his head buzzing. There was a hand at his collar then and he was hoisted back into a kneeling position before a terrific kick lifted him up and smashed him back down on his shoulders. He opened one eye and saw the man step astride of him, he saw the punch start and then felt it land across the bridge of his nose, followed by two more in rapid succession. There was a kick to his ribs that rolled him onto his side and he tried to focus beyond his rapidly swelling eyes to find Charlie, but couldn't see past the dust being raised by his own beating. The buzzing in his head had grown to a roar and he managed to croak out a curse before something hit him in the back of his skull and the world went dark.

It took the gunmen only a few minutes to gather the herd and begin to move them north across the river and into the wilderness that lay between there and the docks at Punta Gorda. Henry and Charlie were left, horribly beaten and unconscious, in a palmetto thicket near the trail. The cattle were never seen again.

VII

Upon reaching Colonel Harts landing, in Palatka on the return trip upriver, Bull wasted no time in drawing his wages and gathering what few personal possessions he owned. Naturally, the Colonel had tried to persuade Bull to change his mind and remain on the river, but Bull had made up his mind to travel south with Carter. Saying goodbye didn't take too long and borrowing a canoe from the Colonel, they began their trip farther upriver toward Lake George. The canoe would be left with the trader post on the lake and would reclaimed by plantation employees on their next visit to the post.

They had traveled about twenty-five miles south of Colonel Hart's landing before coming to the mouth of the Oklawaha river which runs windingly down state in a generally southwesterly flow toward the old military outpost of Fort Brooke. At the convergence of the two rivers the pair navigated between whirlpools and cross currents. Bull sensed his friend growing a bit apprehensive about canoeing in the turbulent waters.

"Tis nothin' to be gettin' all round eyed about. We'll be surviving this trip I'll wager. You just relax and before you know it the current'll be a might friendlier. I can tell you've not been to keen on ridin' in this hollowed out log, but for the places we'll be passing, it's the most efficient way to travel by far. Before we're to be reaching that post on the lake, we'll be travelling through the narrows where the channel shrinks so that a man can nearly reach out to touch the bank on both sides of the craft. It's here that the treetops overwhelm the sky in places and keeps the woods dark about you. It's along these stretches, that you'll be needing to keep that funny looking gun of yours handy. But, don't let me be puttin' your mind to worryin' for no reason. I'm sure God will see us through safely lad. If you don't trust in me lad, at least trust in Him!"

They traveled all day long and a good bit into the night before reaching Lake George. They turned eastward and skirted along the edge in near total darkness. Neither man wished to enter out upon the open water in the dark, so they continued along the edge amongst the croaking of a million frogs, and the plentiful grunts and groans from unseen gators. Near midnight, Bull whispered to Carter that they should tie up for the night an approach the trader's post by daylight, lest they be mistaken as renegades out for no good. They tied to a long row of low growing willows, having decided to spend what was left of the night aboard their small craft rather than risk stumbling about the bank in the dark. After no time at all Bull's snoring was joining the myriad of night sounds echoing all about them. Carter, as was normal for him, found trouble getting to sleep, so he determined to remain awake and alert for as long as possible. Into the wee hours before dawn Carter awoke with a start, surprised that he'd actually dozed off. He thought idly of his folly at attempting to remain awake all night, then grew instantly alert as he realized that the normal sounds of the night had altogether ceased. Carter looked toward his companion in the rear of the canoe, to find his form still stretched out as he had been the last time Carter had given him notice, but he was too aware that the mans snoring was as silent as the night. Then, from the lake shore, past the willows and in front of their canoe, a light shuffle in the leaves ten no more. Carter was immediately aware to the unseen presence onshore and ever so slowly retrieved the carbine from between his legs on the canoes bottom and prepared himself for whatever might happen next.

Seconds passed and rolled into minutes as the men lay unmoving and defensively alert. Soon the bugs began to sing and before long the frogs took up the tune and the night resumed with its usual chorus of wild sounds. Both men remained alert as the darkness began to give way to the approaching dawn and as light gathered upon the surface of the lake Bull finally broke their silence with a cautious whisper.

"D'ya hear it Carter?"

"Yes, I did. Directly to my front, but I've not heard it leave. Have you?"

"If you'll keep that carbine on the willows, I'll untie us and paddle off into the lake and away." Bull suggested.

It was then that a soft voice called from the shore.

"Hello the boat."

Carter swung the muzzle of his carbine to cover the spot where the voice had come and called back.

"Good morning. Who is hailing us?"

"My name is Jim Billie. I am Seminole and you tied up near my camp in the dark. I am armed but wish only for peace. What say you?"

"Carter Holder is my name. I too am armed, but travel in peace as well. I come to the traders post here on the lake."

"It is early to bother the trader. If you will come around the willow thicket to your left, you will see my dugout. I welcome you to breakfast. I come to trade as well and we can go on together after a meal."

"Thank you, I'm coming in." Carter called to his yet unseen host. "There are two of us in the boat."

"I know, your partner snores as loud as a bull gator growls. Come in, I have plenty." Jim called back.

They turned the canoe as instructed, and sure enough, not fifteen yards from where they had tied up in the dark, the willows opened up and there lay a rustic looking canoe filled with clay pots and leather bags, beached on the shore before a small cluster of water oak and hickory. Jim Billie had seated himself upon the prow of this canoe with an ancient musket crossed over his lap and smiling warily. He was dressed in leather leggings and moccasins and went bare chested, but for a cape of woven grasses he wore about his shoulders. He was a handsome man of the same age as Carter and held himself proud when he rose to greet them. Carter and Bull landed their canoe alongside of Jim's and followed him over to a small fire, shaded from the lake by two limbs from a sable palm. Over the fire, Jim had a pot containing a thick gravy and nearby the fire, wrapped in green palmetto leaves were a dozen biscuits baking golden brown.

"I did not intend to startle you this morning, but I had to know with whom I was being visited, before I made it known I was here." Jim told them apologetically.

"I understand that well enough," Carter agreed. "but why not alert us last night, we could have moved on."

"I heard you arrive and tie up last night, so I knew you were not coming ashore. I knew too that my fire was well hidden and in the dark you could not have seen my dugout, so you did not know I was here. Not knowing the type of people you were, I did not want a conflict in the dark, although the advantage was mine. I waited awhile and went over to investigate you. Your friend here had been snoring for a long time before you slept yourself. That is when I came closer to see you, when I foolishly broke a stick beneath my foot. At the sound, your friend stopped snoring, so I stayed remained still." Jim said nodding toward Bull.

"When you awoke as well, I knew I had alarmed you, so I sat down and waited." Jim finished.

"I'm glad you invited us to breakfast, but why not let us pass?" Bull asked. "We may not have ever known you were about."

"Because, when you began to talk in whispers, I knew I had made you uneasy. I thought it best then to let you know that I was about. And as I've said, If you are going to the traders post, you needn't hurry. He tends to be a bit gruff in the mornings and does not enjoy being disturbed before breakfast. His post is only two miles that way, along the shoreline." Jim indicated with a sweeping hand.

"These biscuits are remarkable Jim, I've not eaten them before. Is this a type of sour dough?" Asked Carter.

"That is coontie bread." Jim explained.

"We Calusa dig the root often. Our women dry it and pound it into flour for cooking. It is very good to cook with. I have a lot in my dugout, that I am bringing the trader. I can spare some to trade with you if you like." Jim continued.

"We've nothing to trade with," Bull spoke up. "we're delivering this boat to the trader and hoping that from there we can find passage South to the Caloosahatchee river. That is in your land Isn't it?"

"It is, but why go there? The trip is long." Jim asked.

By the time Carter had finished his story, they had eaten and were preparing to go to the trading post when pushing his dugout into the lake, Jim turned and said.

"It is good that we met today. Now we may see what course will lay before us." Then began to paddle away, leaving Carter and Bull to follow.

Both men admired the ease at which the Seminole guided his rough looking craft over the waters of the lake as Jim Billie stood in the middle of his dugout and paddled along with slow even strokes. They traveled along the waters edge where willows often gave way to great stands of cattail and sawgrass, fronting wetlands of bald cypress and bay. Upland along the shoreline was a mixture of oak, pine, palmetto, and long stretches of elderberry. Farther inland could be seen the stately hammocks of live oak and magnolia, glowing handsomely in the light of the still rising sun. In the distance, a small dock protruded about ten feet or so into the water and Jim was guiding his craft toward it. From the dock the land sloped upward a ways toward a small cluster of palms beneath which was located three small square buildings made of rough hewn lumber. Near the buildings was a small empty corral with a lean too shelter for housing tack. The ground all around had been worn to dirt and an equally worn path ran up from the landing where the three travelers now beached their canoes.

As they approached the buildings along the pathway, the door of the center structure opened wide and a man with a familiar look about him, stepped into the morning light. He was clad in a bright yellow, loose fitting shirt hanging low over dark gray breeches and sported a red woolen cap, the style made famous by French trappers over the last hundred years or so. A great big smile crossed his face and he greeted them warmly.

"Welcome friends, welcome to my post." Then upon recognizing the Indian, his smile grew broader. "Jim Billie! I've waited for weeks for you to return, I thought perhaps you'd taken a wife and was home growing fat. I'm glad to see you've returned. Who are your friends Jim?"

"My names Carter Holder Sir, and this is my friend Bull. We're traveling South toward the Caloosahatchee river country and your brother Jason in Jacksonville advised us to stop by here on our way." Carter said stepping up and grasping the fellows hand tightly.

"Well, you know Jason eh? How's he getting about?"

"I was with him last week and he looked healthy enough. He said that he'd be looking forward to seeing you soon. He offered me a job poling barges on the river for Colonel Hart and now that I've fulfilled my obligations to him and the Colonel, it's time to be continuing south again." Said Carter.

"I know the man well and I can say this too, you do have the look of family about you. I'd have guessed you to be brothers, had I not already known. I worked for the Colonel and Jason for some time. I only recently left their employ for to follow this lad along and the Colonel asked that I leave this canoe here with you. He'll be sending a party along to fetch it along with some business they'll no doubt be needing with you." Bull offered while greeting the man with a firm handshake himself.

"That'll be fine, we can pull it up out of the water and turn it over there in the brush so it won't hold water. I expect it'll be there when they come to get it." Looking around Ray asked. "Bull, I don't see another canoe though, just how do you two plan to make it farther upriver without one?"

"I'll take them." Jim spoke up to both Bull and Carter's surprise. "I was asked by headchief Calusa to hurry back from my trading route. There is unrest among the people of the Caloosahatchee and I should not have left, but I had promised the coontie flour to you. Now I think I was sent here to bring these men back with me. The cattleman Floydd will be pleased."

Carter's brow raised at the mention of his uncles name and he studied the the indian a moment before asking. "How do you know my uncle?"

"There will be time for that later, now we have business with my friend Partridge." Then motioning for the trader to follow, he turned back down the path toward his boat.

Bull whistled low and asked with wonder. "Isn't this some turn of events?"

"My Ma used to say that the Lord works in mysterious ways. I wonder what trouble he's talking about with the people along the river and how he knows my uncle?" Then turning to Bull, "We're only a day and a half away from the plantation and I have a funny feeling about what that indian just said. I have no idea what we're heading into and if you've any second thoughts about this undertaking, I'll understand."

"First off," Bull spoke up. "you'll find that I finish what I start regardless of how the trail might wander. And the second thing is, don't be calling it an undertaking; it sounds too prophetic."

After leaving the Lake George post, the river narrowed a bit more and ran that way for a good many miles. Travel on the river was easy, but the darkness of the river as it ran through the narrows kept Carter on edge as he sat in the front of the dugout paddling against the current. Often they would enter parts of the channel where the trees of either bank grew together in a tunnel of green. Wild grape grew in such profusion here, as to block the view of the surrounding forest and offering protection of the thousands of tiny birds which had made their home in the natural arbor.

Little talk had taken place since leaving the post earlier this afternoon and although Carter was dying to hear of the trouble which involved his uncle, but he did not ask. Instead he waited for the indian to tell it when he was ready.

Jim sat mostly silent in the middle of the dugout, paddling expertly and only now and again speaking to offer instruction to his new wards. Bull was situated in the rear of the craft, but rather than paddling, he trailed a pair of fishing lines behind the dugout catching panfish for dinner. Upon reaching a relatively open area of high ground along the water course, Jim directed Carter to help beach the craft and they set about preparing camp for the night. There were no other travelers on the river that they could see, but the remains of many campfires scarred the ground along the waters edge giving testament to the wisdom of the campsite. While Jim and Carter set about the camp preparations, Bull built the fire and was soon cooking a meal of coontie biscuits and fresh caught panfish.

As the trio awaited their meal, in the gathering darkness, Jim broke his silence and began to tell of the troubles he'd given hint to that morning.

"You asked me if I know your uncle. If you wish to know, I will tell you about him for I've known him for many years. He is family."

Carter and Bull moved closer to the fire and gave Jim an attentive audience.

"I was young of age when removed from my clan by the older headchief Calusa who wanted certain of our young men to become educated in the ways of the white men that were coming into our lands so that we may have proper dealings with them. I was proud to do this for Calusa, but I missed my family very much. I was sent to the fort at the mouth of the Caloosahatchee to attend the Christian school and learn what I could. I was permitted to return home on occasion, but I had a room behind the stables where I stayed most of the time. It was not a bad place, but I was never at home there. I remained at the school until I was twelve years of age. I enjoyed watching our Sun return to sleep and set on the waters where the ships tied up on the long wooden dock. One evening that I went down there I was stopped by a man who spoke neither English or Seminole. He had been there buying cattle to take away somewhere. I still do not know where, but it was a large ship. He stopped me as I walked to the dock and a girl he had with me asked if I wanted a job feeding his cattle on the ship. I did not. He spoke some harsh words and called me indian. I turned to leave and the man grabbed me and was taking me to his boat. I fought him, but he was strong and I was yelling to get away. The girl, who was a little younger than me, started crying and telling me not to fight him or he would hurt me. I was young, but I am Seminole, I fought hard, but still I was being dragged to the man's ship. There were people standing around the dock, loading or unloading other boats docked there. There were cattlemen in the stock yard tending their cattle, but I saw no one who would help. I began kicking and biting the man and he began to hit me with his fists and I fell to the boards. He cursed me wildly and kicked me in the stomach. I was hurt and could fight no more, but I saw the man pick up a piece of a broken crate to hit me with it. I closed my eyes, so I never saw the oar that hit the man on top of his head. The yelling stopped, so I opened my eyes and I recognized one of the cattlemen that had been to the fort before. He was standing over the body of the man who had attacked me. The girl came to me crying and she helped the cattleman take me to a doctor.

"It turns out that the man was from Cuba and he had purchased the girl in that country as a servant on his ship. It turned out though that this Cuban man was a fragile man, because the strike with the oar killed him. The man who came to my rescue was your uncle. I was Seminole and people felt surely I was responsible for the mans death so I was not permitted to return to school. The girl had nowhere to go, so he took us both upriver to his ranch where he and his wife nursed me until I was strong again. They gave a home to the girl in exchange that she help around the house and he escorted me back to my clan in the Big Cypress. Headchief Calusa appointed him as a member of our clan and he is now my uncle too."

"That would make us cousins then. That right?" Carter asked.

"And so I take you to our uncle. He will be happy I think." Jim answered.

Carter was quite surprised to hear all of this and wanted Jim to continue.

"That's quite a story, Jim. I must tell you though, I've never met my uncle before. He and my Ma used to write each other regularly, for holidays and such, but he's not aware that I'm coming. Once a long time ago, he invited me to join him, and I'm coming in hopes that I still will be welcome." Carter said.

"Jim, Bull and I have been wondering about the trouble you reffered to. What is it that's going on down there?"

Bull began removing their food from the flames and setting it on individual palmetto leaves to cool as Jim began again.

"The troubles began after the federal troops reoccupied the Fort Meyers. They brought with them men who survey lands, make maps and charge taxes in Washington. The tax man comes to say that Uncle Floydd owes big money for land. They say he has no rights to land he bought from my fathers, father, until he send big money to United States Government. He has paid in the past and he pays again now. Still not good enough, so he gathers herd to sell at fort to pay more. He sends them to the fort with my cousins Charlie Jumper and Henry Osceolla, but the cattle never reach the fort. Charlie and Henry have not been seen. The news come to the village by runner when I left to make my trading route. Warriors left to help find them, I do not know any more. News travels along the river of men from the North coming to claim his ranch. He has some help, but his heart is not strong and he will need more help if a fight should settle the matter. That is why you've been sent here. You will make the difference. The Great Father is wise to bring us together, don't you agree?"

Carter nodded solemnly as Bull reached for his portion of dinner.

"Well lads, I don't know if our trip is divinely inspired or not, but I have never run from a fight. This Irish blood heats up quickly I tell you. Now I'm glad I bought this little shotgun from trader Partridge. I may be needing it to secure that job. Eh, Carter?" Bull spoke with pride of his new Greener side by side twelve gauge.

"Eat up now my fellows, my belly button is near about to rub a blister against my backbone and I'll not be denyin' myself any longer."

Carter received his portion and ate in silence while reviewing all he'd just learned. One thing was for sure, this trip was quickly becoming quite an adventure.

VIII

Early spring had begun to feel more like late Summer as the sun passed it's crest in the noonday sky. The heat was exhausting and the ever present dust cloud kicked up by the activity in the fort's compound created a most uncomfortable environment for Buford Fettterman as he sat nearby an open window of his unkempt little office. He had grown to hate Florida since he had arrived, assigned to the state by his superiors, four months earlier. He already had endured the warm snowless winter, fighting off mosquitoes and sand flies, only to be punished by the stifling spring weather. If this was any indication as to what Summertime held in store for him, he knew that he must do everything in his power to return northward to his home in Washington with it's crisp spring air and vibrant colors. Money was the only obstacle and Buford knew his only out lay in the deal he'd struck with those darn Bostonian carpetbaggers for the B3C. If this deal would fall into place, he could return home with his share and live in comfort. Who knows, he may even find another wife to keep him, maybe one a bit more tolerant of his many indiscretions.

He wiped at the sweat which was forming around his neck and cursed, again, the miserable weather when a knock sounded at the office door.

"Come in." He called out to the unknown visitor.

As the door swung wide he saw none other than JD Floydd step into his office followed by that pretty young lady he kept at his ranch. His heart tightened in his chest as they entered the room, scared that he might be coming to pay the debt. He rose to greet them.

"Come in, and welcome Mr. Floydd. Welcome to you as well Miss." Buford greeted them with a wide grin and an outstretched hand.

"I was just thinking of you JD. I expected you in any day now to close the books on that tax debt. I'm so very glad you made it in. Now we can put it all behind us." Buford bluffed a little, feeling out the old man.

"Well, thanks. I'm glad to see you too Mr. Fetterman." JD said slowly.

"Please JD, call me Buford."

"Thanks, Buford. I'm not in here today to pay that debt Buford. Josephina and I came in here today to the fort to check on two of my drovers that have come up missing. I sent them here to the fort driving a small herd of beeves to sell. I intended to use that money to pay the six hundred dollars you say I owe the government. Now, almost a week has gone by and I hadn't heard from them, so I came today to find out what's become of them. You wouldn't know anything about it would you Buford?" JD asked flatly.

"No, I assure you. I've not seen the first cow pass through here this week." Buford lied, cautiously.

"Well, after speaking with the Captain of the garrison and the brokers over by the docks, no one else has seen them either. The herd is the least of my concern though. My two drovers have disappeared as well." JD told him.

"I'm troubled to hear about this, did you know these men very well?" Buford asked him with mock sympathy.

"If your asking if I think they taken the herd from me? No! I've known both of then since they were boys. I'd trust them with my life any day, much less a few head of cattle. I sent a rider south to the Calusa villages to see if any news of them had reached the tribe, but I'm worried about them Buford. Something bad's happened to them and I just can't imagine what." JD said with worry in his voice.

"You think rustlers?" Buford kept up the lie.

"Perhaps. Sure I lost a few head here and there over the years to drifters and such, but I've never lost an entire herd. The captain is sending a telegraph to the other military outposts to keep an eye out for the brand, but can't offer any more help than that." JD sighed heavily and his features softened as he looked directly into Buford's eyes.

"Here's the problem I now have. You've collected all the real money I can account for and without the sale of those cattle, I can't meet the deadline you've given me for the rest. Can you give me an extension or perhaps a line of credit or something?"

A prickle of excitement coursed through Buford as he heard the old man admit that he was broken.

"Credit? No, Mr. Floydd, I'm not authorized to extend any deadlines beyond their time limits previously established. Why, if I did that for you I'd have to make the same exemptions for every landowner in the area that neglected their tax duties." Buford stopped and shuffled through thick leather bound ledger on the desk before him.

"According to the records, I served you the notice of your late penalties in the amount of six hundred dollars right at three weeks ago. You've still got a week to gather more cows. That's plenty of time right?"

"No Buford it's not. I've been sick and now with my drovers missing, I'm short handed by two. I need more time, just one more week and I'll pay you in full. That'll give me time to conduct a roundup and drive in those cattle myself." JD pleaded his case.

"Mr. Fetterman," Josephina spoke up for the first time. "He's not a well man. The doctor says he shouldn't be working, can't you help him?"

"I'm sorry Miss, my hands are tied. There are rules and tax laws in place that I must abide by." Then turning back to JD, he continued. "Sir, after this week expires, your debt to this country must be raised to twelve hundred dollars. I've explained to you before Mr. Floydd, what happens thirty days beyond that. I am sorry, but there is no other way."

A red glow was forming in JD's face as his anger began to rise. "I come here to ask you for help. Can't you realize what I'm telling you? I raised that herd. I'm doing everything I can to meet your deadlines. I'm short handed, worried about my men and all you can do is threaten to double my debt and take away my ranch. What kind of man are you?"

"I'm an employee of the United States government and I have a job to do whether it's popular or not, the tax laws demand enforcement." Buford said quite dryly.

"You can get mad at me if you wish, but the fact remains. You have a debt which is owed. Your options are to settle it in a timely manner or not. Regardless of any health issues or hard times plaguing you, you've got thirty seven days to bring payment in full to this office or I will be forced to file your land as forfeit and it will be sold. A new title will be established for the new owner and you will be removed at the discretion of the purchaser. Now, if you'll excuse me Mr. Floydd, I have work to do."

That said, Buford rose and escorted his visitors to the doorway. JD remained silent as he led Josephina out the doorway and into the dusty compound. She turned and looked back as the door shut behind them, then looking back at JD, noticed the redness was fading and his face was growing more ashen. He'd had that same look when he had gotten sick the last time. She walked to the wagon with him and once he was seated she asked him to take one of the powders the doctor had given him. As he swallowed the medication with a swig from their canteen, Josephina gathered the reins of the little black mare and they started home.

"You know, we'll be fine. There's plenty of time to raise the herd we'll be needing. The Captain as much as guaranteed that the fort would buy up to two hundred head and that's more than enough. If you like, tomorrow I can go to the reservation for more help." Josephina tried to comfort him as the little wagon creaked and groaned over the uneven ground.

"Go alone? I should think not! You have no idea what became of Henry and Charlie. Do you really think I'm going to let you go anywhere without me? You and I have to stay together, we have to keep an eye on each other." JD gave her a nudge and a smile, then took over the reins.

"We'll get the help girl, I'm not too worried about that. The money will be paid and then no one can tell us we can or can't live here on our own land. Momma Luanne and I are to old to be starting over some place else. What's weighing on my mind is Charlie and Henry. If bandits had killed them, then likely we'd have come across their bodies, or at least spotted a buzzard. And if it was bandits come down on them, It seems strange that it would happen now when we've never had that sort of problem along the river before. I can't help but think their's someone behind it all trying to keep me from paying off those tax debts. I can't help but think it. Mostly though, I worry about the boys. I shouldn't have let them go it alone. I should have waited and went with them myself."

Josephina put her head on his shoulder as they rocked gently along the trail toward home.

IX

Two more full days of travel along the St. Johns brought them to a wide bend in the river with a noticeably western bending shoreline. The time passed easily while traveling with their new guide and Carter and Bull took full advantage of every opportunity to question him about JD and his cattle ranch. They were following close to the shoreline which was overgrown with cattails and palm until Jim pointed out large stake that had been driven into the river's bed. The stake had three painted stripes and a cluster of blue jay feathers dangling from the top.

"That is sign for trading route. The trail leads across to the Kissimmee river. We will camp here then use the canoe for a sled to cross the land." Jim explained the marker and set the dugout toward a cut in the shoreline.

"How far is it to the next river?" Bull questioned.

"Using the dugout to carry our supplies, four days. Then you will see that we shall travel faster. The Kissimmee runs to the South, as any river should. Traveling with the current, we will be to the lake on Okeechobee by the end of the week."

The overland route was grueling. Jim picked the way along the traders route, but Carter could not distinguish any markers to follow. They took turns dragging the dugout and many times they found themselves carrying it across the wild tropical landscape. The land as lush and fertile, certainly it had never known the plow and Carter found himself excited by the opportunity to farm this wild tropical landscape. Certainly the ground was capable of producing crops because all around him he was surrounded by magnificent green growth.

They traveled along mostly quiet, but for the occasional curse of a missed step or from contact with the many prickly vines and cactus that relished the sunlight of the more open flatwoods where travel was the hardest. Carter much preferred the shade of the hammock and the open areas cut off from the sun for it certainly made easier walking. Each night the trio camped in secluded campsites that held remnants of previous camp fires, which gave confidence to Carter that Jim was still on course, although many times he'd suspected the man to be lost, but dared not question him about it.

By the evening of the third day they were nearing the river and Jim snuck up on and killed a small gator sunning himself on a mud bank beside a cypress pond. The fresh meat was a pleasant treat from the hard tack and coontie bread they had been traveling on.

"This tastes a lot like the snapper turtles my brother and I used to trap on the Flint river back home when we was kids." Carter observed after having tried the gator's tail meat for the first time then asked. "Do Seminoles make a steady diet out of alligator Jim?"

"Not in the past because there is so much more game to be hunted that is easier to catch. Lately though, our men have been hunting gator for the prices white traders pay for their skins. It is only reasonable to eat the meat from them unless we risk angering the spirits. It is not wise to waste what we have taken."

"Spirits?" Asked Bull. "What spirits would those be Jim?"

"The spirit gator. Each animal has its own spirit that observes the way that we treat its brothers. If we loose respect for the animals that provide for us, the spirits will take them away. That is why as a hunter, when we take a life for our own use, we say a prayer and make an offering. It does not have to be much, but not to offer anything is to offend the spirits. Many hunters carry tobacco to bury at the site and some bury a piece of hair." Jim explained as best he could.

"When you killed the gator back there, did you make an offer?" Carter asked interested.

"Of course I did. There is no other proper way."

"What was it you offered?" Bull wanted to know.

"That is between gator and me." Jim said, tiring of the conversation.

"Didn't you say you were educated in a Christian school at Fort Meyers? Yet you still believe in spirits? I mean no offense, but I am curious, are you an Indian or a Christian?" Carter said almost apologetically for asking.

"I am both. While in the Christian school, I learned to read and I read the Bible often. We learned of Jesus and all that came before him. I learned to walk and act as the white children did when I was among them. I was proud to do this. But before I was educated to your ways I was Calusa. In that, I have no shame." Jim said matter of factly, effectively ending the conversation.

On the water again, the dugout raced along with Southern flowing current allowing the travelers good speed as they floated past some spectacularly beautiful wilderness. Wildlife was remarkably abundant along the watercourse. Deer, bear, gator and hundreds of small animals could be spotted with a sharp eye into the forest on either side of the rivers channel. The bird life was even more spectacular. They passed numerous rookeries of ibis, heron and stork that not yet had attracted the attention of the plume hunters. Busy little limpkins and purple gallinues kept busy in the shallows alongside of spoonbills and curlew. Cormorants spread their wings to dry on most available deadfalls and eagles and osprey competed for airspace above the river, often diving with definitive results as they regained their flight grasping a still wiggling bass. So wild and beautiful the land appeared to Carter that he knew that even without a job with his uncle, he would never leave this land. All about him was fertility and growth, the type of land a man could tame and prosper on. It seemed no small wonder why his uncle never returned to Georgia.

Bull had been spending a fair amount of time riding in silence and Carter began to wonder if the tropical grandeur of this Southern part of the state was having a similar effect on him as he himself was feeling. Carter didn't have to wait much longer though, to find out.

"I know now why yer people fought so hard to keep the Spanish out of here. Once a man builds a history in a place such as this, I can't see him giving it up easily at all." Bull spoke to Jim with reverence to their surroundings.

"Do you know of the Seminole wars Bull?" Jim asked.

"Only what a man picks up in conversation. I've met a few Seminole traders, such as yerself. They've not gone out of their way to educate me. I do know that throughout the wars yer people never surrendered and that was against the same army that just whipped the Rebs. I'll allow ye that ."

"That is true we have never agreed to terms of surrender. Our warriors are fierce when they have a reason to be. I was a small child during the second war when Osceola was killed. However, headchief Calusa tells of the battles from time to time. He is a fine storyteller. In truth though, our warriors killed far fewer of the soldiers than did the land itself.

"Soldiers! They did not belong here and Florida never allowed them to feel welcome. They came and took and destroyed and burned and cut and in the end, they died. They wasted away for their meat did not keep. They did not know how to live with mosquito. A very large number did not see brother moccasin until it as too late and they soon were all sick. It is told that many of the people felt sorry for the soldier for they bore such misery, but could not help them.

"From the day the Spanish man Narvaez cut the nose from Chief Ucita of Calusa island, our way of life has been attacked, now we adapt, we learn your ways. It is not possible to return to the past, therefore we will remain as we are for as long as we can and continue to adapt when we must." Jim finished and the three rode along in silence each carried along with his own thoughts as they flowed comfortably along with the current.

Days were spent on the river and occasionally they would come to where the channel widened to form enormous lakes whose names sounded wild and exotic to Carter. Names like Tohopekaliga, Hatchineha and Okeechobee. The latter though proved to be absolutely immense and at times upon the surface of the lake, the far shoreline was not at all visible, sitting in the dugout. Once they had arrived on this lake, Jim had guided them through hundreds of yards of cattail and sawgrass fields until they gained the open water where Carter spied the first watercraft he'd seen since entering the Kissimmee river. Out in the far distance Carter spied a small sailed vessel with a wide flat looking bottom making its way outward from them and far to the East a long barge was being poled along by a crew. Its decks were loaded and Carter watched as the crews walked the walkways with their long poles.

"Look familiar to you does it?" Bull asked Carter in jest.

"Yes, it seems to strike a memory somewhere." He responded with good humor.

"Aye, it does for me as well. But, all of that is behind us now. We're to be rich cattlemen before long, eh?"

"Let's take one thing at a time Bull. We haven't even got the jobs yet."

"He will hire you." Jim broke in. "As I've said, it is meant to be, you have been sent here to help. He will hire you."

Jim stood up and rode the dugout for awhile, giving directions to his two propellers. He searched the horizon for a good hour, before satisfying himself on a landmark and they began directing all of their energy into reaching the spot of shore before nightfall settled upon them while they remained upon open water. Dusk was rapidly gathering as the dugout passed over the gray surface of the last hundred yards of open water and Jim directed the craft toward a small opening along the shoreline. He explained that the mouth of the Caloosahatchee was close, but they must rest here for the night and he got no argument from either of his exhausted companions.

Morning greeted the three men as they ate heartily what was the last of the coontie bread and sharing the remaining filets of last nights catfish dinner. Carter sensed that for the first time on the voyage, Jim felt secure in his surroundings because, when he made the breakfast fire, he made no attempt to conceal the smoke or flames from and passers by. Also, there was no rush about him to be on their way before full daylight. Once or twice, he even caught Jim smiling to himself.

"Jim," Carter asked in good humor. "you're in a good spirit this morning. What's the occasion?"

"I am coming home. In two or three more days, I will sleep in the chikee of my family, upon a bed prepared just for me. I will tell all the stories of the journey and especially how the great spirit honored me by trusting me to lead you here. Shouldn't a man be happy to once again walk the ground of his father and his father's father? I think so."

"Are we on that ground yet?" Carter wanted to know.

"We slept on Calusa land last night. Our territory begins Westward at the edge of the great lake Okeechobee toward the gulf and South through the everglades and the Big Cypress Swamp."

"How much farther until we reach Carter's uncle's place?" Bull queried.

"Maybe today, perhaps in the morning, who is to say?" Jim answered.

"Well, It'll be soon enough I expect." Then eating the last bite of his coontie bread biscuit, changed the subject by adding. "Jim, you make the most wonderful biscuits. I can't tell you enough how good they are."

"It is the flour that you find the flavor, not in my cooking." He said pleased that Carter appreciated the food.

Then with a more serious tone Carter spoke again to his Indian friend. "Thank you Jim."

"You are welcome, but do not carry on so. For they are the last we will enjoy until reaching Uncle Floydd's ranch. His Mrs. always keeps a jar of coontie flour in her kitchen."

"Not just for breakfast, Jim. Thank you for bringing us this far to Uncle Floydd. No doubt we would now be lost in the wilderness without you."

"That's right Jim." Bull joined in. "You've been a gift I tell you, a rare gift."

"It is the way it is supposed to be. The cattleman needed help. Now you are here. Is it a coincidence that our paths crossed at the same time and in the same place in this entire world? No, it is not. Is it also a coincidence that there may be a fight gathering and you are experienced in combat? No, it is to be." Jim stated plainly, as a matter of fact.

"Perhaps, but how do you know I was in combat during the war? I never spoke of it."

"There are some things which a man does not need to say. Your eyes tell your story. You are yet a young man, but your eyes have the tired look of an old man who has seen too much. I see the look in many faces traveling South. You are no different, am I right?"

"I suppose you are." Carter said as Bull stood by with a thoughtful air about him.

That evening after a day of fast padding with the current and not stopping for lunch, they arrived at a sun bleached cypress landing which held fast two small river barges made of rough hewn cypress planks and was encircled by a chest high split rail enclosure. Upon close inspection, Carter rightly guessed they were for transporting small numbers of cows on the river. Above the dock and supported by two waist thick pillars was a weathered plank board sign bearing the inscription.

"BIG CYPRESS CATTLE COMPANY"

And beneath that, in smaller letters was written.

"Jefferson d. Floydd - B3C"

They beached the dugout by the landing and stepped up to the worn path leading inward to the ranch house in the distance. It had taken Carter many weeks of travel to get to this place and now a jolt of indecision coursed through him as he stood on the soil of the ranch he had so wanted to reach, but his mind strayed to his brother Seth and his new wife. He hoped he hadn't been a fool to leave them.

X

Jim led the way along the trail which wound upwards along a low sandy ridge, through low growing scrub oak and palmetto, toward what Carter hoped would become his new home; at least for a while. In the distance, a few head of lazy looking brindle cows, stood watching the new arrivals with little interest. Carter could just make out the B3C brand on the flank of the nearest. The terrain was mostly open, much more so than that which they had been traveling past. The land on which the main house had been built was high and allowed a good view of the pastures that spread out from the river. It was surrounded by a cluster of buildings and small corrals set near the cover of a pair of ancient live oaks, the occasional mature cabbage palm and one lone sable towering above it all. The cover of the trees aided in deflecting some of the Summer heat while also helping to block the cold North winds during Wintertime.

The house was of the same design as the one he'd seen at Colonel Hart's plantation. It had the look of planed cypress and had been built along the Northern edge of the tree cover, facing south toward the tack shed, barn, and stable. Off to one side of the barn was a sizable low roofed structure which was used for a bunk house. A clover leaf shaped corral had been erected behind the stables and tack shed. Six small and dark marshtackie ponies were resting in the corral, which had been made of split railing.

There was a covered breezeway that led from the back of the house toward the outbuilding which served as a kitchen. Outside the kitchen door was a large triangular bell, similar to the one Carter's Ma had used to call in workers at mealtime and as Jim led Carter and Bull in amongst the ranch headquarters, an older lady stepped from the kitchen and began ringing away on the dinner bell. She was a handsome lady, full figured and with soft brown eyes. Her dress was faded from one too many washings and was protected by a large white apron, with a pair of oversized pockets sewn on the front. Once she spotted the trio arriving she stepped down into the yard and greeted them warmly.

"Jim, I'm so glad to see you. You're just in time for supper too." Then turning toward Carter and Bull, "And who do we have here Jim?"

"Carter Holder Ma'am, I'm your nephew down from Georgia and this is my friend Bull." Carter spoke up.

"Aye, I'm very pleased to meet you Ma'am. Collin O'Hara is my Christian name, but Bull will do if you please." Bull bowed formally while removing his hat.

"Well, I'm Luanne Floydd. Please come on up to the porch, my husband JD will be along shortly. Mr. Holder, did you say you are my nephew?"

"Yes I did. My mother is JD's younger sister."

"Of course you are, I've heard of you all many times, I'm just so surprised to meet you." She said covering her mouth in surprise. "JD is going to be so glad to see you here. Is your brother coming along as well?"

"No, he's married now and runs the farm. Ma and Pa are with the Lord now so I thought to come and ask Uncle JD about a job."

Taking Carter's hand she led the way up to the broad porch and ordered them all to sit while she ran back to the kitchen to check on her stove. She had a good many questions that she wanted to ask, but thought it probably best to wait until JD arrived and had a chance to visit this young man. As she removed the last of the supper from the stove, she couldn't help herself, but to smile. These men were arriving at such a time surely was a blessing.

They waited on the wide porch, Bull commenting happily about how orderly things appeared to be. In a short time horses could be heard arriving and They looked to see a small group of riders approaching from the South. An older man led the group, comprised of three Indians with flowing black hair and an teen boy covered in oversized work clothes. The old man stopped short and dismounted upon sighting his visitors upon the porch, and handing his reins to one of the Indians, stepped forward to greet them. He was a thin, angular old man dressed in a faded blue shirt and well worn canvas breaches. His walk was a bit stiff, but he mounted the porch with authority and with a nod toward Carter and Bull, greeted Jim with great affection.

"Welcome back Son. You're looking fine." He said taking the Indians hand.

"Thank you Uncle, I'm glad to see your well. I have men here you want to meet." Jim spoke of his two companions while still holding the man's hand in a firm grip.

Carter stepped forward and thrust out a hand.

"It's really good to finally meet you Uncle Floydd. I'm Carter holder, your sister's youngest."

The old fellow returned the handshake and searched Carter's face for recognition. Carter tensed beneath the pressure of the unyielding gray eyes that appraised him and seemed to finally find recognition.

"So...you are." He said with a smile beginning across his weathered features. "I'm JD and I am proud to get to meet you too. You do have your fathers look about you, that's for sure. I invited you to join me here a few years ago, is that why you've come here?" He asked to the point.

"Yes sir, it is. I should have written ahead, but after my discharge from the army, I was of a mind to travel. I hope I'm still welcome."

"By the grace of God, yes! Of course you are." JD declared with a wide grin. "And, who's this gentleman here?" He asked turning to Bull.

"I am a friend of Carter's and an unemployed traveler, hoping you'll have room for me as well."

"As long as the sun rises and sets, there'll be plenty of work to go around. I can't afford to pay a weekly wage, but I can offer your bunk, some groceries as are available, and a share after the cattle are sold. I know that isn't a lot, but it's all I can afford. I hope you will stay."

"It would appear then, that I am no longer unemployed. I thank you Sir." Bull said with much enthusiasm.

"Jim, please show this man where to store his affects while I get to know my nephew, eh?" JD asked, pointing toward the bunkhouse. Then to Carter said. "Have a seat here, we've some catching up to do."

JD was terribly disturbed by the news of his sister and her husband. He had many questions about them, but Carter could only reveal what he himself had been told. They talked long into the night about family and how Carter came to be there on the ranch. Carter had many questions of his own, but saved most of them for a later time. Uncle Floydd was not at a loss for words and Carter gained quite a bit from just listening to the man speak. Luanne served their supper to them on the porch, so that they could continue to learn about each other. She could hear JD begin anew as she returned to the dining room.

"Carter, I came to this place in August of eighteen hundred and forty-one. I homesteaded this land. I filed papers on about two thousand acres of tropical wilderness which after several years of hard work and planning became good enough to support a heard of cattle as to make raising them become profitable. Once the land upon which I originally settled was improved enough, I attempted to file papers on a large tract to the South. The government had deeded that land to the Seminoles right after they built Fort Meyers down river. So, I sent word to the tribe that I wanted to purchase the land. I received an invitation to meet with the head man, who sold me a grant of an additional four thousand acres, to the South. Now, many years later, the land cleared and the grass became sufficient to hold a sizable herd. I had a steady market to the army post. The Quartermaster was a Captain Winfield Scot Hancock. The same one that became so famous after Gettysburg. Any way, between him and the buyers from Cuba, the ranch did fairly well.

"Once the war started, President Davis authorized the garrison to buy every bit of beef they could to supply the army. Cattlemen all up and down the coast made out well from the demand. I'm not proud that I profited from the war, but business was business. The one thing that protected me was that I never accepted the pepper money the new government was so fond of, so they paid me in gold and silver coin. From what the Yankees occupying the fort again tell me, that paper money from the Reb's aint worth a red cent these days.

"Now, all of it is gone. The Yankees took it all back. They're always coming up here with some debt or another they claim I owe. They're really tight on the reins. It was good days when them Rebs was in the fort though. Now the best of the free life is long behind us now, I hope the good times aren't really over though, for good."

That was the only hint of trouble JD volunteered that night. He did continue talking on about the ranch and explaining how things ran. He talked of the daily goings on and of the three Indians he had currently working for him and how more were usually available during the Spring roundups and Autumn drives.

"I noticed the three Indians that rode in with you, but what of the boy that rode in?" Carters question caused his uncle to laugh.

"Why, that's no boy. Her name is Josephina. She's been living with us here for quite a number of years now. She's kind of the daughter we couldn't have." He spoke, still finding humor in Carter's mistake.

"Jim told me of a girl when you rescued him on the dock; that must be her then?"

JD's smile fade a bit and he began to explain.

"Jim told you all about that eh? That was a long time ago. I had sold a small herd that morning and was coming from the purchasers office when I heard this Spanish fellow bellerin' like an old bull. I look over and see he's about to beat some skinny kid to death. There didn't seem to be nobody makin' much of a move toward steppin' in, so I went over and whacked that Spaniard with a paddle that was handy. You see, I didn't mean to hurt him, but figured I had to stop him or the kid was gonna die. I hit him over the head and he went down hard." JD took a breath and shifted his seat a bit, growing uncomfortable in the memory.

"There was a girl there also and she had been cryin' and beggin' the man to stop and after I knocked him down, she helped me lift the boy up. That boy, as you know, was Jim and she, Josephina. We started him back from the dock and I wanted to take him to a doctor as fast as I could when I heard someone say that I had killed the man.

"Jim had been going to school there at the fort, but after the fight, the school assumed that because he was an Indian, he must have been the cause, so they wouldn't let him stay once the doctor had cleared him. Josephina had been purchased as a maid for the sailors quarters, from a madam in Cuba. She was young. She begged me not to put her back on a boat, so

I brought her and Jim home with me. It wasn't long before he went back to his village and Josephina has stayed on and thank God for that. She's been invaluable in helping Luanne around the kitchen and now that she's older I have a heck of a time keeping her out of a saddle. Truth is, she can ride, rope and herd as well as any cowboy I've ever hired.

"The constable came around with a few questions, but they was enough people down on the docks that witnessed it and satisfied him I did no wrong."

They sat for a moment listening to the night sounds when JD spoke again. It's late, you'd best come on in the house and I'll show you a room you can use. There's already a bed in there and you just make yourself comfortable. We'll be up early tomorrow, I've got to gather a herd to be driven to the fort. We made a couple of runs today to see where the cows were going to be in the morning, so finding them shouldn't be much of problem."

Carter smiled and followed his Uncle into the house and to the bedroom he was directed to. Afterward Carter had his usual trouble finding sleep and as he lie in the dark looking forward to his first day of cowboying.

A gentle breeze from the river was flowing into the room through the open window, fluttering the curtains and bringing a soft song to his ears. He slid quietly from the bed and slipped out past the front door and listened to the sweet notes hanging in the dew laden air. Off across the yard, by the stables bathed in moonlight, was the girl. Josephina was her name. She leaned on the top rail of her ponies stall and sang her low, lonely melody to it.

Carter listened for a few minutes and began more than once to leave the porch and go over to introduce himself, but in the end, his decision was to go back inside to his bed, still listening to the lovely voice that echoed around his soul.

XI

The new day started quite early on the B3C, and Carter quickly dressed and joined the small gathering along the breezeway leading into Aunt Luanne's kitchen. He was pleased to find Bull looking well rested and as excited as himself. He gave him a pat on the shoulder as he walked past to join his uncle who was just receiving his breakfast through the serving window of the kitchen.

"Good morning Uncle JD!" Carter exclaimed with the high spirits of a child in a toy store.

"Back at you Son! Did you sleep well?" He asked, turning to meet his nephews grin.

"I rested plenty. Now I'm ready to get started earning my keep, so to speak."

JD chuckled and as he found a spot to sit and enjoy his breakfast assured Carter, "Don't worry, you'll earn it. Not being saddle broke yet, today may prove to be quite a chore for you. Now get on over to that window and get yourself some breakfast, Lunch aint for another seven hours, so eat up."

Lanterns had been hung on either side of the doorway to the kitchen and in the weak light, Carter made out the forms of Jim and the three other Indians just off of the walkway eating their morning meal. With the exception of Jim, they all wore roughly the same attire as would be expected of a cowboy. They sported multi-colored patched shirts over canvas work trousers. The older of the trio went barefoot while the other two were shod with low healed riding boots of the type he himself had on. He hadn't been introduced yet and thought of going over, but instead he received his plate from Aunt Luanne and settled himself on a rough bench beside JD and listened to the smacks, clacks and grunts that seemed to make up the Seminole's language.

JD interrupted the lively conversation that was building between the four Indians and asked Jim his plans.

"Jim, will you be joining us awhile or do you have to be getting on back?"

"I must go this morning. Headchief Calusa asked me for a quick return and will be expecting me. I shall not let him down, although I wish I could stay longer. I am glad to be with you."

"You know I'd like nothing better. I haven't thanked you yet for bringing these two tenderfeet down state for me. I do thank you." JD said and then remembered. "Also, tell Calusa I hope to see him soon and I wish him good health."

Jim, almost as if being cued, picked up his rifle, adjusted his woven cape about his shoulders and after nodding toward Carter and a quick word to the Indians, he disappeared back into the darkness toward the river.

JD looked over at Carter and Bull as they finished their breakfast and spoke in good humor.

"Well, I see you two don't mind rising for work. We don't always start so early, but it's bound to be a hot day and I'd like to get as much done as we can, while it's cool yet."

"I've never found it agreeable to waste daylight I must say, there is no way to know how many days the Good Lord may see fit to grant this humble Irishman so I'd better use up as much of the ones I have." Bull offered, bringing a chuckle from them all.

"I was raised on a farm Uncle JD. I'm used to early mornings. What will we do to start this morning?" Carter queried.

"In the far southern section of the ranch there's a creek that runs fairly true, from east to west. That's Lost Dog Creek. They's some pretty good pasture greening up down there and last evening we located quite a few head grazing on it. I only need a hundred or so beeves for us to start the drive to Fort Meyers. They won't be giving us much trouble once they're rounded up, but getting them out of them bay heads and what palmetto thickets there are will give you a full days work." JD sipped his coffee and asked them both, "Ya'll ever crack a whip before?"

Carter shook his head no and Bull echoed the response.

"I'll be glad to teach them if you'd like." A female voice called from the kitchen.

Carter turned and for the first time noticed the girl standing in the doorway of the kitchen. He knew then why he had mistaken her for a boy last evening. Her hair was pulled up beneath a battered and oversized cowboy hat that long ago had lost its shape and sat squarely on her head. she had on a boys loose work clothes; an old gray shirt under a pair of overalls faded to the color of a late Summer sky with patches spread across both knees. The clothes showed about as much figure on her as a sack of grain. What he most noticed, as she stepped forward into the light was her large expressive eyes. They were dark, almost black even and they captured his gaze without a hint of shyness. He judged her to be in her early twenties and marveled at the transformation from the nights siren to the cowhand before him.

Carter stood as she approached and with some difficulty managed to speak.

"Good morning Josephina." Seeing surprise in her face, he quickly added, "My Uncle told me."

"Good morning to you Carter." She returned with a smile and emphasis on the name. "Your aunt told me." She said nearly teasingly.

"I'd be glad to teach you two how to use the whip if you'd like. It's not that tough once you get the hang of it and it sure does help to get a stubborn cows attention."

"Thanks, I'll look forward to the lesson. I'm sure there's a few things you can teach me." Carter offered.

Josephina looked him over from head to toe and uttered. "No doubt!"

Carter watched her walk past him and off toward the stables and felt himself blush hearing the soft laughter at his expense, coming from those around him. He finished cleaning up his plate and hurried to join the others as they headed through the dark morning for the stables to saddle up. He and JD were the last two to get their mounts ready to ride. Bull had already made his way astride a runty looking little black mare and JD had picked out a leggy bay stallion for Carter to ride named Gator who came along with a warning from JD.

"This one's a spirited horse, you have to show him each morning that you'll be the one in charge. He likes his tricks, but he's one smart herder. When a cow makes a break, you just give him his head, he'll do the rest."

Just then Josephina rode alongside of them and gave her opinion.

"Maybe you should walk him around a bit before you try to mount up, he's a little rough right off."

"I'll be fine," Carter said getting a little red at a girl giving him directions. "you've ridden him haven't you?

"Sure, I've been riding horses like him for most of my life, but I like my horses spirited. Beans aint beans unless you've put in some seasoning." She called over her shoulder as she moved her horse out into the yard.

Carter wasn't sure what that was supposed to mean, but didn't ponder it further as he turned his attention to his uncle.

He watched JD give a few soft words into the ear of his horse, then grasped the reins and some main hair in his left hand and the saddle horn in his right. He swung himself up and into the saddle with a fluid motion that belied the old fellow's truc age.

Trying to emulate his uncles actions, Carter grabbed a hold onto the horse and lifted himself up, but Gator never let his right foot find the stirrup. The horse took a couple of long jumps sideways that bounced Carter right into mid-air. He hung there for moment before crashing into the hard packed ground and knocking half of the breath out of him. He pushed up on his hands and coughed from the dust of the stable.

"You have to get up and try again Son. You can't let O'l Gator think he won. I told you he was playful in the mornings." JD called to him.

Carter heard the undisguised sounds of laughter coming to him from the yard, but the one that grated his nerves was the high pitched giggle that could only belong to the girl. He rose stiffly and returned to the horse who stood still this time and he mounted without further incident. His uncle was smiling.

"You done real good Carter. Always get right back on! I've seen men before that wouldn't."

Nodding his thanks, he started the horse into the direction that the rest of them was heading. Although he didn't show it, he was grateful for his uncles small compliment. The dark of the early morning was beginning to lighten in the east as the sky took on a rosy hue. Bull fell in beside Carter and his uncle as they rode southward toward Lost Dog Creek. As they bounced along in the saddle, JD began to explain what was expected of them during the drive.

"You two follow along here till we get to the creek. We'll string out along the near bank before starting the push toward the open pastures to the North. Lost Dog Creek runs pretty much East and West, coming out of the Big Cypress Swamp.

Once we reach it we'll make a turn and start dropping off riders along the way. The last man at the end of the line will, which will be me, starts the rest with a crack of the whip. Sounds easy enough doesn't it?"

"When we start out, how fast do we ride?" Bull asked him.

"Well, it aint no race." JD told him. "Just let the horse do most of the work. That little gelding your on has worked more cattle than I care to recall. He'll find his own pace, but listen to the other crackers driving down from you. If you think your getting too far out ahead, pull him back some."

"Why is it that you use the whips on the cattle?" Bull queried the cattleman.

"There's some of these old scrub cows that take a notion that they'd rather hide up in a thicket or clump of palmetto rather than move on and there aint nothing better to get them going again when you need them too."

"So it doesn't hurt them?" He asked further.

"Not really." JD tried to explain. "You don't want to hit the cow with it. Mostly you can pop it over his head or in the brush beside him and that moves them pretty good. Only every now and then do you come across a real stubborn one that you'll have to crack, but their hides so thick, it only stings them bad."

Carter had been riding along listening to his uncle and Bull when he finally spoke up.

"Uncle JD, I was wondering about something that Jim said on the way down here. Do you mind if I ask you a few questions?"

He watched JD as a look of discomfort spread across his face and Carter was about to let him off the hook when JD forced a smile and nodded.

"Sure Son, spit it out. I'll answer as best as I can."

"He spoke of a stolen herd and two Indians that worked for you disappearing. Is there something more you can tell me of that?"

"Yes, Henry and Charlie." He began to explain, "They were taking a small bunch of cows to the fort for me a few weeks ago when they were jumped. They showed up at their village on the reservation. They both had been beaten pretty badly, but they'll survive. The cattle's gone, but that's the least of my worries. They were taking fifty head to Fort Meyers to sell so that I could meet some danged tax debt the Yankee's are saying I owe. I rode to the fort to check on the cows, but the captain at the fort said they never made it in and that's why we have to raise this herd. I usually don't like to gather until farther along in the spring on account of some of these cows may be pregnant. Any real stress can cause trouble with the calf being born. But, I can't wait any longer. I have to raise the money."

Carter thought on it a while then asked.

"The last herd, you say, was fifty head and this morning we're to gather over a hundred. Why so many more?"

"Taxes!" JD raised his voice in disgust. "I've paid my taxes Son. But, for the last six years I was making payment to the Confederate government. Now the Yankees are back in the fort and this tax agent from Washington is come along saying I owe the Union six years of back taxes. Now here's the thing, I paid my debt with the gold I'd been getting from selling cows to the Rebs. Next I get served notice that I owe late penalties for the tax amount. I refused to pay it and they said that they could auction off the ranch for the amount and that I'd be given the boot. So, I raised a herd to cover the amount. You know now what happened to that.

"Talk at the fort is that there's some folks kinda behind all this hopin' that I won't meet the deadline for the payments so they can scoop up my ranch for a song and that that's who helped themselves to that herd. Well, I didn't make that deadline so they doubled the amount and gave me an extra thirty days. That's why I need to sell twice as many cows. If I don't meet this next deadline they can double it again. Then thirty days later I'm sold out.

"I pleaded my case at the tax office and as well to the captain at the fort, but he can't interfere with another branch of the government. From what I hear along the river, It's like that all over the South these days. I won't even consider losing my land, so I'll pay whatever I must. I just want it over with.

"Now boys, we're getting close to the creek now. Bull you drop off first, then Carter and Josephina will be next in line. If you have any trouble, just do what she does and you'll be fine." JD paused and asked. "Any more questions for now?"

"Just one." Carter said deeply serious, "Do you know who these people are that are behind all of this?"

"No. Just talk along the river is all, but the tale I hear the most is of two Yankees coming down to buy up land for farming sugar cane. It makes sense, that they'd be interested in this ranch. All of the land is already cleared. It's in my gut that whoever they are, they're behind the bunch that jumped Charlie and Henry." JD grew quiet and Carter bothered him no more with questions, hoping to save the old man that aggravation.

They rode along in the growing light of dawn. The temperature was quite pleasant now, but promised to climb much higher as the day progressed. Carter studied the whip hanging from his uncles saddle horn. It had a wooden handle about eight inches long and braided rawhide that was tapered down the length of the whip. The end had a small leather flap and a piece of waxed cotton cord attached. It looked to uncoil to about ten or twelve feet in total length and he looked forward to seeing it in use.

JD turned and spoke to him in a businesslike manner.

"Carter, I'll be leading this procession along the creek, so I'll ride on up front. It won't be much longer and we'll be getting there." JD touched his spurs to the stallions flank and he surged up ahead of the line of riders.

They held their horses to an easy trot as they followed JD to the creek. Carter noticed Josephina up ahead riding alongside that big shoeless Indian and wondered if that had been her idea or his. Not that he really cared, he reminded himself, he was just noticing.

He was already sore from the fall he'd taken that morning and with the bouncing of the saddle, would have bet they had traveled nearly twenty miles before they reached the creek. Bull claimed it was closer to two.

Josephina dropped back and joined them as they neared the creek.

"How ya'll doing so far?"

"Faring well Lassie, I've been astride a horse since I was a wee lad back in Davenshire of mother Ireland. This is the first I've ridden for some time I admit, but the feeling comes back quick. The bones remember." Bull answered first with a beaming grin causing Carter to wonder if Bull was pleasured by the riding or by the attention of the pretty eyed cowpoke before them.

"I'll be needin' to get used to this saddle." Carter said, hoping that he didn't reveal too much of his discomfort. "After all the marching in the infantry, being atop of this horse is a bit foreign." He said with a smile.

"Well, you got right back on this morning." Josephina smiled sweetly. "That says something for you. Before long you'll be setting in that saddle as easy as a rocking chair."

Upon reaching the creek, JD turned his horse East and the Indians followed him single file. Josephina pulled up on the bank and turned toward Bull.

"You sit right here. When you hear us begin the drive, just walk your mount back over the trail we came in on. If any cattle try to cross around you, head them back toward Carter and myself. He'll be a hundred or so yards down the creek here and I'll be another hundred or so down myself. Okay?"

"I'll be fine darlin', you'll find me to be a fast learner." Bull told her with that same beaming grin that made Carter chuckle a bit despite himself.

Josephina gave him a high spirited giggle and turned her horse to go drop Carter off at his position up the creek. It was only a few minutes after being positioned that Carter could hear the whips begin cracking down stream, indicating that the drive had begun. He looked far to the left and saw Bull start his little pony forward and looking right watched Josephina uncoil a whip from her saddle horn as she started forward as well. He was paying her attention as she started swinging the whip about over her head in lazy circles, like a lariat, then bringing her arm down sharply, caused it to crack as loud as any pistol he'd ever fired. She noticed him watching her and she gave him a little wave before cracking again. His mount had already started forward through a stand of widely spaced trees with incredibly dense underbrush. The horse was picking its way along, following a narrow cow path through the thickest tangles of vine and scrub when the ground to his front rose up with a great crashing as two brindle colored cows erupted from their morning beds. Carter gave a start and caught himself, just before toppling out of the saddle. One fall this morning was already too many!

The two cows continued along the trail in front of the pony with a slow step until joining another one a little farther up. Far to his right a small group of four or five cows rose up and started in the same direction. A young Bull broke from a cluster of cabbage palms and palmetto and pawed at the ground while bawling his objections. Josephina rode over and cracked her long whip into the ground a couple of times behind him, which prompted him to fall in line behind the others quite tamely. Cows were moaning and bawling their discontent all up and down the line in front of the riders. The whips began cracking at regular intervals and Carter kept his eyes on Josephina as she swung her whip expertly here and there, urging the cows along. They pushed on for a couple of hundred yards through scattered pine dotting a broad stretch of knee high palmetto flats, through thick pockets choked thickly with low growing scrub oak with the hateful prickly pear cactus and on through strips of dark forest beneath live oak and hickory until reaching one of the large open pastures. Carter entered the open behind his small gathering and turned to watch as cows and riders appeared from the treeline and he marveled how their timing had kept them all pretty much abreast to one another. The cleared area seemed a bit over thirty acres and once the riders were all into the open they began to gather the cows all together, well out into the open until all of the cows were gathered into one dusty, noisy herd.

Bull come riding up to join Carter and spoke cheerfully. "I think I'll be liking this ranching Lad. It's less work than poling the barge over the river and think of it. We're being paid to ride a horse! Cowboying! That's a fair occupation if I do say so myself."

"I see you two didn't get lost!" JD had ridden close and was calling to them. "That's encouraging. Now, you two stay back here and we'll double back in case there's some we missed on the first run. Just relax and keep this bunch together. They're pretty well settled to feeding, but watch them just the same, we won't be too long at all."

"Don't worry, we'll watch them." Carter called as the other riders fell in behind JD and headed back into the brush. The three Indians each gave a quick nod and a smile as they rode past and Carter sought to catch Josephina's eye, but she went on about her business and galloped away with the others.

The cattle had all settled down and were milling about now, feeding on the new shoots of springtime grass that just was beginning to peek up from the ground. Bull slowly drifted over to the opposite side of the bunch and sat back a ways, not wanting to crowd them. They appeared to be quite content to shuffle around grazing, but Carter kept a sharp eye on them just in case one decided to try to make a getaway.

Off in the distance, back toward the creek, the popping of the whips began to sound off again announcing to them that the new push was underway. The sun had climbed well into the sky by now and sweat had begun to break out enough that Carter's shirt was becoming completely soaked through in places. He wiped at a trickle as it made it's way down the back of his neck and looked around, surveying the landscape. He could only imagine the amount of hard work that went into claiming this stretch of open pasture from the tropical wilderness that preceded it. Surely after so much work, there could be no doubt that JD would fight to the end to keep it. Now the he, himself was involved, he would certainly fight if called upon and his mind wandered back to the two Indians that had been ambushed. He knew there was potential danger waiting for them on the drive to the fort and was proud that he would be along. JD looked tough, as tough as any he'd met so far and the Indians had a look that suggested they could take care of themselves. But, the girl certainly had no place in a fight and how much experience the others had in such matters, he did not know. He had been in many skirmishes in the past few years and figured one more battle, one way or another, couldn't hurt.

Soon the riders drove through the treeline with a much smaller group that was quickly mixed in with those of the first gathering. JD rode past, dust covered and sweaty, and directed Bull and Carter to follow along while the two booted Indians looked after the gathered herd then led them all much farther down the creek to begin a new drive. As they rode Carter took notice of the young woman almost hidden beneath a cowboys clothes and found that to the knowing eye, she was absolutely lovely astride her pony. She truly seemed in her element as she rode along during this new push, swinging her whip and expertly guiding her pony here and there, intercepting the occasional cow, attempting to evade her an Carter felt he could watch her all day.

A cow and calf leaped onto the trail ahead of Carter's horse and the mount lunged forward to intercept them. Carter winced as the sudden start increased the level of discomfort which already had been building all morning. He could feel the grimy sweat between his rump and the saddle and all along the insides of his thighs where the leather rubbed. The salt from his sweat set up a burning in that region that grieved him no matter how he shifted his weight or tried to ignore it while watching the girl.

"You doing okay there Carter?" She called to him with a mischievous grin crossing her face. "You look as if your getting a bit sore in the seat. It happens to most tenderfeet until they're broken in."

"Actually I'm doing fine. I'm even having fun." He called back, a bit annoyed that she could spot his discomfort so easily.

"It's just that you seem to be shifting your weight around a lot from side to side. You can spot it every time with new riders, but don't worry, you'll toughen up quick enough I bet." She trailed off with a laugh that was echoed by the big shoeless Indian that somehow had made his way to her side again.

Carter felt a little heat rising up, but he just set his jaw square and prepared himself to endure the rest of the roundup without complaint. Carter's horse continued his pursuit of any wayward wandering cows and he began to appreciate the horses skill and training. He noticed that the horse was always alert and would align his ears with the cow it suspected to try an escape. It was as if the horse could predict a cows movements before they actually occurred.

The sun continued it's climb into the sky and the day continued to grow warmer. As the sun reached it's mid-day peak, Carter worked alongside the other riders as they merged a new gathering into the sizable herd they had posted in the pasture. By the time the group had finished this latest drive, Carter had spotted his Aunt Luanne working about a little wagon hitched to another of the small black ponies. Lunch time had finally arrived.

They ate and rested in shifts and during the break from driving, Josephina made good on her offer to teach Carter and Bull how to crack a cattleman's whip. The first time or two Carter brought the whip around behind his head and streaked it forward to crack, he actually caught a part of his ear. He couldn't find it in himself to admit to the girl just how much that stung, but with a little more practice he was clearing himself and doing a fair job of cracking it. Bull seemed to be a natural with it and was soon experimenting with the whip enthusiastically. After awhile he returned the whip to Josephina and joined Carter beneath the shade of a small oak growing along the pastures edge.

"Already, I'm glad I came here Carter and before I forget, I want to thank you for bringing me here. Like you I'm growing a bit sore from the saddle, but 'tis to be expected. I'm a long time out of the saddle. I was a wee lad back home when I learned to ride. My father was a ferrier and I practically grew up on a horse and I haven't forgotten how, just my body needs to toughen up a might."

"Why did you ever leave Ireland Bull? What brought you here?"

"Tragedy struck my family and I had no reason to stay, but that's a story for another day. Right now it looks like your uncle is about ready to mount up again. We'd better join him so he don't think us shirkers." Bull said humorously as they started for their horses. Carter's horse, Ol Gator, stood as still as a statue for him to mount, much to Carter's relief.

Aunt Luanne was noisily packing the little wagon as JD rode over to them with instructions for the afternoon drive.

"Boys, we'll hold this herd here and start making drives through those cypress hammocks to the North. We always find a few head hiding away in there from the heat. Bull, you follow Josephina an Paulo" JD said while nodding toward the girl and her ever-present, barefoot companion. "Denny and Egret will hold the herd here until we get back." He nodded toward the two Indians sporting riding boots. "And you come with me." He said to Carter, then spurred his mount into action and headed toward a long line of cypress trees in the distance. Carter fell in behind him and watched as Bull pulled up alongside Josephina and couldn't help but feel a bit jealous.

Sure enough, after entering the dark, stagnant confines of the cypress strand, they did find cows. Carter would have preferred to have dismounted and walked through the thick cover of the strand, but JD remained astride his mount, then so did Carter. It was no fun pulling the cows from the thick dark cover. JD's whip kept a steady beat as Carter fought to avoid the clawing branches and prevent himself from being swept from the saddle, should the horse lunge after an escaping cow. Soon the ground began a slight rise and they exited the first strand with about a half dozen agitated cows and moved them farther out along a pine flat, bordering the pasture. JD asked him to hold the small gathering there amongst the pine and palmetto as he returned to the cypress cover to search for stragglers. When he returned from his second sweep, they moved the cows out onto the pasture and mixed them in with the mornings herd and continued on in that manner until the evening came and they had gathered just over a hundred head into the pasture.

The three Indians were to stay with the herd as the rest of them rode toward the house to spend the night. They all were quite tired from the long days work and were covered in dust and dried sweat. The discomfort Carter had been experiencing was reaching new levels, but he told himself to ignore it a bit more, at least they were headed toward the house.

Once back at the stable, they unsaddled and tended to the horses needs before going to wash for supper. As he stepped from the stable and awkwardly began walking back toward the house, Josephina came up to walk beside him.

"I was a little hard on you this morning with the teasing and all, but you did real fine today." She smiled sweetly as her compliment caught Carter a little off guard.

"Why, thank you. I tried to follow your example all day." He said a bit bashfully.

"I have some balm for you in the house to rub down with tonight. It'll take out some of that soreness and get you ready for tomorrow. I'll get it to you so you can rub down before supper."

"I'd appreciate it. I'm afraid I'm a bit out of shape for this kind of work, but I should heal up easy enough. I had the same trouble with my feet when I first joined the infantry. After a few thousand miles of marching though, they got broken in real well." He assured her.

"So, your a soldier?"

I was, but first I was a farmer. My father taught me to nurture the land and reap a good harvest. The army taught me to march across it and destroy things."

"Which are you now?" She asked him as she looked up at him with her dark expressive eyes.

"Neither. But who knows, I may become a cowboy if I get enough practice." He joked lightly then nudged her shoulder. "I've a pretty good teacher in you don't I?"

"I don't know if I'm a good teacher or not, but I'll share everything I know with you."

"One things for sure. You're the prettiest teacher I've ever had." He added, hoping not to seem to forward.

"If I can help, let me know. Just try not to fall off of your horse again okay?" She let out a quick giggle then took off to get the medicine she had promised him.

Carter stepped up onto the porch where JD and Bull were cleaning up at a wash stand Luanne had provided for them. Josephina had disappeared inside the house and Carter waited his turn to wash. JD stepped back from the basin and began drying his face on a towel that had been hung over the porch rail.

"I was wondering Uncle JD. About Josephina, is she spoken for?"

JD began to laugh and Bull put on a silly grin as JD responded good naturedly.

"I see it didn't take her long to get you going huh?"

"I didn't mean nothing by it. I was just wondering." Carter said, with a mild blush.

"No, she's never married or anything like that. Oh, there's been many offers, but always from drifters comin' up and down the river that stop in for a bit of work or a meal. She never has taken a shine to any of them so far. Who knows, she might not be the marryin' kind. Nothing wrong with that I guess. Fact is, I've never talked to her about it. Maybe Luanne has, but I never have."

"I'm surprised at you Carter." Bull said, not wanting to waste a good tease. "If I'd have known you were to be so romantic, I could have put in a word for you with Lillie Mae back at Hart's place. You have to admit, she had a lot to love an could cook too."

"No thanks, I'm not ready to wear no wedding ring just yet. I was just wondering is all and you two shouldn't read too much into it okay?" Carter said trying to save his pride.

He stepped up to the wash basin and started cleaning up while ignoring their taunts and thought to himself about her singing the night before and how much he'd love to hear her again this night.

Talk at the table was minimal while everyone hungrily attacked the platters of food Luanne had prepared for them. There was stacks of grilled beef steak, fried squash, mustard greens, and coontie bread. Outstanding! As the contents of the platters before them began to dwindle, conversation eventually picked up. Mostly, talk centered around the days activities, with a few chuckles at Carter's expense thrown in here and there. He took it all in good naturedly, but his attention focused when Luanne made mention of the heart condition his uncle had recently developed.

"JD, did you have any trouble today during the roundup?" Luanne asked with a suddenly serious look in her eyes.

"No, of course not. I had good help out there today, even if some of it were a bit green it was good help just the same. The horses all worked well and the cattle were cooperative for once. No trouble at all." JD said lightly, but she wasn't ready to give up yet.

"I'm asking about your heart, did it act up at all?"

"No, and I expect I'd have mentioned it to you if it had. Now, I don't expect my nephew and our good friend here want to talk about the infirmities of an aging cowpuncher."

"Yes I do!" Carter said soberly. "What is it that's bothering your heart?"

"He had a spell about a month or so back, nearly scared us all to death." Luanne answered him.

"Hush now woman, I'm okay now. I haven't been sick since that one time and the doctor gave me the medicine for it if it happens again. Really Carter, there's nothing to be worried about." JD told him dismissively.

"I watched him all day Ma'am." Josephina spoke up for him. "I watch him close, you know that. If he looks to be overdoing it, I'll cut him back some."

"See, I've got a guardian angel riding herd over me, what could go wrong?" JD asked with a wink of conspiracy toward his adopted daughter, but Luanne still wasn't satisfied.

"But, your guardian angel won't be going to the fort on this drive." Then turning to Carter and Bull asked them. "Will you two please keep an eye on him for me? He's awful ornery at times, but I love this old fart and don't want anything to happen to him."

"Don't worry a bit me lady. I'll watch him as if he were me own sweet pa!" Bull said comfortingly.

Carter started to speak, but was interrupted by Josephina who had become quite alarmed.

"Why won't I be going to Fort Meyers? She asked wide eyed.

"It's already been settled between Luanne and myself." JD waved her off. "Your to stay here and look after the ranch until I get back. There may be trouble on the drive and we can't bear the thought of you getting yourself hurt. It's final, so don't bother arguing about it!" JD told her firmly and Josephina deemed to go slack under his stare and she resigned herself to stay home. Next he cast that same look of seriousness toward his new employees.

"Also, you two. Your new here so I will not ask you to come along. If you'd not mind, please stay here and look after the women folk. I'd be mighty thankful."

"No way Uncle! I may be new to this ranch, but I could never sit by as kin went into harms way. Fact is, I've already given this possibility a good deal of thought and if these people are bound to stop you from reaching that fort, you may be needing me along. I've been under fire many times and I'm a crack shot. I'm going Uncle JD, that's for certain!"

"You can count me in too JD! If I'm to enjoy the privilege of living and working on this ranch, I figure then that I ought to put up a fight for it. If nothing else, I'll carry a bit of the ol' Irish luck with us. Sometimes, you just might need a little luck to pull you through." Bull proclaimed.

JD was genuinely moved and grinned his thanks to them both, then suggested that they retire to the front porch with a bottle of something special he'd been holding out for special occasions or snake bites; whichever came first.

XII

Pausing at the head of the four steps that descended to the floor of the hotels main dining room, Phillipe Dabria surveyed the room with approval. He stood before the room with an air of importance, while looking very much the part. His suit was tailored gray broadcloth and his hat was spotless white. His shirt was white, his tie was black and his shoes were black and polished to a mirror shine. Out of sight, tucked in the waist band behind a broad, black silk sash he carried a small double barreled Derringer. When dealing with new clients, such as the one he was about to meet, it paid to be careful. He was handsome and meticulously groomed and before him lay the promise of not only a fine meal with a good wine, but the opportunity to own a controlling share of the largest new sugar plantation in Florida.

He approached the table with the manner of royalty and placed himself before the unoccupied seat across from Mr. William Clinton.

"I trust you had a fine journey *Monsieur* Dabria?" Clinton said, rising to greet the gentleman and shake his hand.

"*Wi, a bon voyage* indeed, *Monsieur* Clinton. So nice to meet you finally."

"And you Sir, I've waited a long time." Clinton said graciously. "I arrived in from the plantation on the Caloosahatchee just yesterday and am so pleased to report to you that things are progressing well. It's proving to be the best acquisition my partner and I have ever made." He lied through his teeth.

"Yes, what of your partner, will he be joining us this evening?" Dabria asked.

"No, unfortunately, Mr. Kennedy stayed behind to oversee the development of the project. I know that you'll have ample opportunity to meet him in the future. He very much is, like myself, dedicated to seeing this venture become profitable for all of our investors." William said while continuing to misrepresent the truth.

"How long do you anticipate before we may expect a return on our investments *Monsieur*?"

"If our yield is sufficient, the investment should become profitable in two years. That's not a very long time *Monsieur Dabria*. You see, eighty percent of this countries sugar is currently being imported from Cuba. There are some farms here in the states, but nothing to match the scale of the plantation we currently have under development. The land is prime fertile tracts that are already cleared and awaiting the first planting. The property itself sits on a major shipping route only four hours inland by river to the Gulf of Mexico. It's as if the almighty Himself picked out the location." William kept on.

"*Monsieur* Dabria, I've offered twenty thousand shares of the plantation on market in Boston for five dollars a share and am holding an additional twenty thousand shares to be distributed amongst our European investors until after this meeting. The price is the same as those offered here in the States, but due to currency exchanges, I must ask that all foreign purchases be made in gold."

"I understand *mon ami* and thank you for allowing me to bid first on this investment. When would you expect to receive the gold?" Dabria inquired casually.

"I am prepared to receive deposits into an account at the First bank of St. Augustine, just down the street from here." Clinton told him. "How about it *Monsieur* Dabria, do you feel like gambling on a sure bet?"

"I am a gambling man and I know that there are no sure bets. However, if it pleases you, I will provide payment of one hundred thousand dollars in gold tomorrow morning and accept all remaining shares of your plantation, *si vous plaire*?"

Clinton sat dumbfounded for a moment, but recovered quickly enough to accept the offer and accept the Frenchman's hand to bind the deal.

"Now, *Monsieur* Clinton, if the business of this evening is in order, please call me Phillipe and we shall *laisser bon temps rouler! Eh, ami?"*

"Absolutely Phillipe, now if you please, call me William and we'll celebrate our new agreement." Clinton said as he motioned for the waiter to bring the first of many glasses of champagne.

The next morning found William at the waterfront attempting to purchase new passage on a vessel bound for Fort Meyers with a world class hangover, softened by the knowledge that by the days end, the Frenchman's gold would be delivered into their account. From here on out, Alford and himself would be very wealthy men. Now, surely, the matter with the old rancher had been settled and they could start hiring crews to begin the planting of cane on the B3C.

XIII

Sleep was not long in finding Carter that night as he lie exhausted in bed from the days labor. Josephina had made good on her promise to bring him some balm for the chaffing along his inner thighs and buttocks. He was quite grateful to her for the medicine although he was terribly embarrassed to need it. She hadn't lingered like he would have liked her too. He would have loved an opportunity to get to know her, but didn't dwell long on the thought as he drifted off to sleep.

Morning arrived with Carter being awakened by his uncle knocking at the door of his little room. He rose sorely and dressed as quickly as he could after applying another liberal coating of the medicinal balm Josephina had given him. he was having quite a time walking, but after pulling on his boots, he exited the room and made his way to the breezeway where he found his uncle and Bull working over their breakfast and received an amusing grin from each as he made his way stiffly to the kitchen.

"Carter, are you havin' trouble with them boots? Cause you look like yer walkin' funny today." JD began the teasing.

"No, it aint the boots." Carter replied while returning the grin. "I just thought that if I'm going to be a cowboy I might as well walk like one. Aint this how you do it?"

"I'd say that you've got it down Son, you're doing just fine."

"Don't worry none Carter, your not the only one ambulatin' a bit funny this mornin' I promise. I know the discomfort your having and I tell you, once we start moving around and limberin' up, we'll be getting along well enough." Bull told him assuringly.

"Good morning Carter." Josephina greeted him as she brought over his breakfast plate.

Carter was so taken by her, that he almost forgot to respond. She wore a light blue, homespun dress with a white apron over the front of it. Her long black hair had been combed straight and hung closely about her shoulders, framing her dark features which took on a soft glow from the light of the oil lamp. Her dark eyes were flashing beautifully and the fullness of her figure nearly left him breathless.

"Is something wrong Carter?" Josephina asked lightly.

"Oh, uh no! Nothings wrong at all. I, uh...well, this breakfast sure does look good!" He finally blurted out and lowered his head to his plate, not trusting himself to look up at her any longer.

"Then eat up." She said. "You'll want to get a good start this morning." She offered him a sweet smile, but he kept his attention on the meal he was attacking and she went back inside the kitchen.

When Carter did finally look up, he noticed JD and Bull nudging each other, both sporting ear wide grins.

"Don't you two start up again." He warned, halfway amused himself, at his own foolishness.

Bull finished with his plate and stood to return it to the kitchen when Carter first noticed that he was carrying the short twelve gauge he'd gotten back on Lake George. He looked from Bull, to his uncle, still seated and sipping hot coffee and studied the handgun, holstered and tied down on JD's right hip.

"I guess you two are ready for trouble eh?" Carter asked growing serious.

"I pray that we won't." JD spoke soberly. "I can't help but think that whoever jumped the boys may still be around and I won't take any chances. Now, we'd better get a move on. We have to bring breakfast out to the boys this morning and we'll get the herd moving while they get a bite to eat. I want to get to the fort while there's plenty of daylight." He rose quickly and poured out the rest of the cup.

Carter dove in on the breakfast and finishing quickly, he waddled out to the stable to join his uncle and Bull. Inside, he spoke a few words to Gator and rubbed his neck for him. The horse nuzzled him a bit and snorted some while he was getting saddled. Carter had not forgotten the lessons of yesterday morning and took his mount for a short walk around the yard before attempting to gain the saddle.

JD had provided scabbards for the saddles, into which Carter had placed his Cattleman carbine with the revolving cylinder. He took notice of JD's scabbard and was impressed to find it housing a new Henry repeating rifle, the kind with the brass action and the lever on the bottom. He'd heard about these weapons, but until now, had never seen one. He'd heard you could load the gun on Sunday and shoot until Friday, so he commented on the rifle to J D.

"It's a .45-70 model. I was needing a new rifle, so Luanne ordered this for Christmas last year. I've killed a couple bucks with it so far. I tell you Son, that's the best shooting weapon, I've ever heard of nor handled and that's a fact." JD told him with pride.

After a few trips about the yard, walking Gator, Carter grabbed a handful of saddle horn and main, slipped his left boot into the stirrup and began his ascent. Halfway up, Gator began a little sidestep dance, but this time Carter was ready and soon he was seated safely astride the stubborn horse. He wheeled around, back toward the tables and caught Josephina watching from the breezeway beside his aunt. She waved and called out to him.

"Nice job with Gator. You're getting better at this already."

Carter returned the wave and grinned proudly. Luanne left the breezeway and carried a pail containing breakfast out to JD to be delivered to the three Indian drovers. He tied it securely to his saddle horn and leaned down for a kiss.

"Don't you worry about me, ol' woman. I'll be fine."

"I will worry and you know that. Just you all be so careful. We'll be praying for you until your home again." Luanne said, fighting back a tear.

JD put the spurs against the flanks of his cow pony and rode swiftly away from the yard. Carter and Bull followed suite and after following along in the dark awhile, they pulled up alongside the old man and rode abreast. The rhythmic plodding of the horses hooves was the only sound until dawn began to awaken the wildlife and darkness gave way to the rising sun. The crickets were the first to sound out their morning salutations, then the croaking of hundreds of frogs opened up from the cypress ponds dotting the landscape. Carter heard a buck grunt from the behind the cover of an elderberry thicket and a tom turkey thundered out his springtime serenade as they rode out to join the herd.

A mile or so before reaching the cattle, Carter finally spoke up about the potential dangers that lay ahead.

"JD, I think it's best if I ride on ahead of the herd aways. If there's any danger, I can evaluate the threat and signal you two to be ready. That way, there's no chance of anyone getting caught by surprise."

"No!" JD shook his head. "I'll not have you ride out alone to meet any danger by yourself. I'll be on point! Paulo, Danny and Egret can do the driving and you and Bull follow me for security. If we face any danger today, I think it best that we do it together. That's what we agreed on last night and now is not the time to be second guessing ourselves." He finished with a hard look toward Carter which stopped any argument from his nephew.

"I just thought I could buy you an advantage, that's all." Carter said apologetically.

"Lad, I know you to be of sound mind and heart," Bull joined in. "but your uncles right. If you were to meet with bandits alone, I would stand a very good chance of losing my friend. Then after getting yerself killed, you would leave us shorthanded to handle the threat. Didn't you learn anything in the army Son?" Bull asked.

"Of course I did, I was just thinking is all. Heck, we may be getting all fired up for nothing, but if it comes to a fight. I intend to take the fight to them. I did learn that the best way to handle an attack is with a counter attack. It causes confusion on their side and can give them a moments hesitation. It's at that time that you must pour it on hot. Do that and you may break their nerve and send the remainders running with their tails tucked." Carter told him.

"Just don't be in any hurry to get yourself hurt Son." JD asked of him. "I like you and I want to spend more time getting to know you, okay? That goes for you too Bull. Please don't take any unnecessary risks."

"Thank you sir," Bull replied, trying to lighten the mood. "I personally see no logic in charging right into battle. That's a young mans way of thinkin'. I, myself, see no reason to be in a hurry. I find that when I take my time and go carefully, I get a more harmonious outcome."

They approached the herd shortly after first lightand found the cattle bedded down together, still out in the open. The three Indian drovers had picketed their horses around the herd and were huddled about a small fire.

JD rode up to them and handed down the pail, Luanne had sent over for them. As the men quickly ate their breakfast, Carter and Bull circled the herd which was beginning to stir about. Soon JD rode over to where Carter was and they watched the Indians get mounted up before they started the herd up and moving with a few well aimed cracks from their whips. The herd rose up bawling loudly and raising dust as it began a slow trek to the North.

"We'll go around that big pond over there." JD indicated with a point. "It'll be a mile or so beyond that where we'll come to the trails head which leads Westwardly along the river to the fort. For the most part it's a good wide trail, but when we reach the narrows, keep an eye out. Paulo and the boys'll handle the herd just fine, so keep your eyes on the woods."

They rode out about a half mile ahead of the cattle and surveyed the scene around them. After a good hour into the drive, they had finally reached the point JD had described earlier as the trail head and they watched as the Indians turned the herd expertly and maintained a steady gait with the lead cows. Carter felt the heat of the friction on his thighs beginning to burn again, but the medicine Josephina had given him was helping quite a lot. The day was still early, though Carter was hoping it wouldn't turn out to be a repeat of yesterdays miseries astride his mount.

The men had fallen silent again as they rode beside one another listening to the soft creaking of the leather, the plodding hooves, cracking whips, bawling cattle and the occasional shout or curse from an Indian. By the time they reached the river, the Indians had the herd stretched out due West and a soft breeze had began kissing their cheeks with the hint of salty air from the gulf. After an hour of travel along the river bank, JD broke the silence and asked Carter with a somber tone, if he could ask of him a favor.

"Of course Uncle JD, what's on your mind?" Carter asked him in as serious a manner.

"It's about Luanne. She's old like me and if something was to happen to me; well, I need to know that there'll be someone to look after her. She'll need someone to run the ranch for her and tend to business. I guess I was wondering if you would consider doing that for me. How about it, would you stay on?"

"I will!" Carter promised with a solemn oath. "I expect you to be around for a long while yet, but if God has other plans for you, then by all means; yes I will."

"Thanks you." JD almost whispered. Then in a more clear tone added. "I know it puts you on the spot, beings we just met and all, but you are family. In fact your all the family I have left around here. I still have your brother and I belong to have a cousin up in Alabama somewhere, but she stopped writing years ago and I don't know what became of her. At any rate, she never bore children. That leaves you and your brother. Josephina has become a daughter to Luanne and me and when we're both gone, I've already prepared it so that the ranch belongs to her, but as good of a cowboy as she might be, it takes a man to run a cattle ranch."

"I tell you Uncle JD, now that you've opened the subject, if I go down hard, will you write Seth and let him know. He'll need to know." Carter looked up to his uncle and received am assuring nod.

"Bull?" JD asked him softly. "If something happens, is there anyone we should notify?"

"No Sir. Anyone that would care about my old bones is already planted back in county Kilkenny of mother Ireland. There's my father and mother an buried beside them is my sister, her husband and their wee child. Across a small walkway is my broth resting near both sets of grandparents and near them is my wife Anna and our wee daughter Nell. Losing them to the typhoid plague is what made me leave and come to America to start over. No, I've nobody to notify.

"I've traveled too far to make it back for burial in that little cemetery. Lord knows I should have stayed, but I didn't and now even though I may come to rest a few thousand miles away, I know I'll be seeing them again, happy as the old days and walking the streets of Glory together." Bull stopped and shook his head back and forth a bit before beginning again.

"If you must though, plant my bones near a shade tree and if the mood strikes you, maybe say a prayer or two, but don't go through too much trouble." He spurred his pony up a little ahead of the others and they let him ride on alone for a time.

Riding together JD became curious about Carter's growing up in Georgia and began asking questions. Carter willingly shared his best memories from home with his uncle and as they rode he told all about fishing with his brother on Flint Creek and the smell of Sunday supper on his mother's stove. He told how Pa taught them to read by an old oil lamp from the family Bible and how he had taught them their nightly prayers. He talked on and on of the old times and paused finally from a sip of water from the canteen on his saddle and noticed a satisfied look on his uncles weathered face.

"Was your Ma happy Carter?" JD asked him.

"Oh yes, she was. I never knew her to have a complaint and the only time I ever knowed of her crying was when us boys left for the war. She and Pa were suited to one another, I guess." Carter noted that his answer made his uncle smile and then thinking about his folks, he smiled himself.

They were passing the hottest point of the day now as the sun rode high in the sky above them. The soft breeze of the morning had disappeared and Carter wiped often at the stinging sweat that made it's way into his eyes and ran down from his forehead. Their shirts were beginning to soak through as they traveled across an open stretch of piney flatwoods which offered barely any shade at all to offer relief from the tropical noon sun. Bull had dropped back to rejoin them and the three were riding abreast when they all drew rein as a covey of quail flushed from the distant treeline they were riding toward.

"Could of been a bobcat." JD offered without believing it.

"Might even have been a fox" Bull said just as disbelieving.

"Maybe it was a varmint, but I don't think so." Carter told them just as he spotted a thin line of dust coming from an unseen rider leaving quickly and he pointed toward it. "There goes your varmint now! Going to tell some other varmints that we're coming I'd guess. We'd best be awful careful from here on out, there's no doubt about it, we'll be having some trouble before this days out."

XIV

As the three riders neared the treeline where the dust cloud had been spotted, the approached with extra caution. Here, the trail narrowed between the river and an ancient cypress head which Carter recognized as a very good spot for someone to have planned an ambush. However, they made no contact here, but easily picked up on the sign left by a single, shod pony leaving westwardly along the river trail.

JD rode back to the herd and alerted the drovers and quickly returned. After riding ahead another few hundred yards a voice hailed them from the security of an elderberry thicket to the left.

"Do not shoot! I ride in peace!"

Carter recognized the voice instantly as JD called back.

"Come on out boy where we can see you!"

After some snapping of branches and swaying of the bushes, Jim rode out of the thicket and onto the trail in front of them riding a short legged, barrel chested marsh pony.

"Good morning Uncle, I thought you and our friends would enjoy my company." Jim greeted them.

"Jim, you beat all! Nearly scared me to death when you called out." JD said with a look of pride at Jim's arrival. "I'm glad you showed up Son. I aim to drive those cows back there on into Fort Meyers and your naturally welcome to come along."

Carter and Bull pulled up close and greeted their friend. Then Jim looked at Carter and asked directly. "Are you here herding cows as well?"

"Yes, I am, why?" Carter asked mildly confused at the question.

"Oh, I thought maybe you were along because of the six men that waiting for this herd to come by, that's why." Jim watched each man straighten in the saddle as he revealed his information.

"Jim, if you know something spill it, there's no cause to be teasing us about it." JD said in reprimand.

"Yes sir, I'm sorry. There are six men though, I've seen them. They made camp along the dry slough below the sandy ridge where the turtles lay their eggs. I saw them just this morning, there was five in the camp, but I'm sure you saw the rider come past this way and it is my belief that he will alert them to your coming and stay with them to stop you. They all carried guns, but they are undisciplined men." Jim told them.

"How do you mean undisciplined, Jim?" Bull asked.

"They have been camped there for two days and never dug a proper hole to bury their own waste. They have not washed themselves in the rivers water and whatever remains of their meals, lies in the bushes about their camp inviting flies and 'possums."

"What do you recommend we do Jim?" JD asked soberly.

"I say drive these cattle to the fort. These are not men that will stop you." Jim said confidently, then turned his pony to join them as they began to take up the trail again.

As they moved up the trail, Carter couldn't stop glancing over at the big Calusa riding near him. Jim had a very determined look on his face and a tight set to his jaw as they rode toward the expected ambush. He was dressed in leggings and wore the same woven grass cape about his shoulders and back. His chest remained bare, but about his waist was an elegant belt made of alligator skin which supported a long barreled single shot percussion pistol and a long, thick bladed knife. Cradled loosely in the crook of an arm was the old fashioned musket Jim had been carrying before. He lacked the war paint Carter had heard of Indians wearing into battle, but was no less a formidable character without it.

When they had ridden to within a half of a mile of the place Jim had indicated as the ambush site, JD held up the procession and sent Bull back to alert the drovers to halt the herd until sent for. Once Bull had rejoined the others JD asked again if any of them had second thoughts. After a moment without a reply, JD and Bull positioned themselves between Carter, on the left and Jim, on the right by the river, and proceeded along the trail at a slow walk searching every bit of cover for danger.

As they arrived at the spot Jim had indicated earlier, a single bandit rose from the brush along the trail-side and stepped into the open and faced the four horsemen with an ugly smirk and a cocked Winchester, butt down, resting on his hip. They neared the man and Carter spotted two others crouched behind a fallen oak about twenty yards off his left shoulder and decided then that when the firing started, he was going to charge that position and eliminate the threat to their flank.

"What right ya'll got to try and pass on this trail?" The bandit asked, directing his question to the old cattleman.

"By the right that this is open range and the only established route to Fort Meyers. Now, I ask you to let us pass friend." JD began to step his horse forward when the bandit began to swing down the muzzle of his Winchester toward the old man, but was interrupted by Jim's long pistol erupting in smoke and flames as it tore a large lead ball through a neat, red rimmed hole which suddenly appeared in the middle of the bandits chest.

Now, for Carter, time seemed to slow down. He saw the flame and smoke belching from Jim's pistol, but before the bandit fell, he already had his horse turned and running straight after the two flankers behind the fallen oak. Smoke began to erupt from behind the log and Carter let loose with a blood curdling yell as he spurred on the mount and raised his weapon as he closed in. One bandit was kneeling with his head and shoulders exposed. The man had a scared, wild look in his eye and fired his gun again and again, throwing his shots without taking aim. Carter's first shot landed squarely on the mans Adam's apple, toppling him over like a doll. As he gained ground on his second man, Carter felt a deep burning rise up in his ribs and yelled out again in defiance. His horse pulled alongside of the log and skidded to a stop, his haunches almost touching the round, right in front of the fallen tree allowing Carter to fire down into his second bandit as the man began to turn and flee. His first shot caught the man in the hip which spun him around facing him again and the next two shots centered the mans chest.

He didn't wait to watch the man fall, instead Carter spun his mount back towards the sound of firing. Reaching the trail bed, he became acutely aware that the burning was increasing in his side and he had a wet sticky feeling all down his side. Bull and JD were taking cover behind a large cypress tree growing along the rivers bank and as he rode past them another bandit climbed clumsily up the river bank and onto the trail in front of him. Carter saw a large knife handle protruding from a bloody wound in the pit of the mans stomach and dropped the fellow with a shot to the head, for mercy or anger, he didn't know, but couldn't reason on that just yet.

No other bandits showed themselves and the firing had stopped. a smoke cloud hung close to the ground about them and singed their nostrils with it's rank odor. Jim stepped back onto the trail, coming up from the river and reclaimed his knife from the new corpse sprawled in the dirt. JD and Bull rode up and took a hold on Carter's reins and tried to help him down from the saddle.

"Leave me be! That's not all of them!" He warned.

Jim called to him then, "There's another floating in the river besides these two on the trail."

"Yes, and two in the trees behind me. Where is the sixth man?" Carter called out insistently.

"Perhaps he fled to warn his people at the fort, but he aint here now, so come down off of that horse Son. Your shot and bleeding now let us help you!." JD cried out to him.

Carter attempted to dismount on his own, but lost his balance and fell into the waiting arms of his uncle and Bull. The pain was now beginning to take over and he felt himself growing faint. Bull cradled his head against his chest as JD tried to stop the bleeding. Jim came quickly with a double handful of river mud to cake over the wound and soon they had the bleeding under control. He tried to sit up. but the pain was now unbearable and he fell back, dizzy from the effort.

JD suggested building a travois to carry Carter along to the fort on and Bull and Jim set about gathering the poles they would need. JD laid Carter's head back down and stood to get the canteen from one of the horses. As he bent over to retrieve his soiled old hat from the ground where it had fallen getting Carter off of the horse, a shot rang out from behind a small cluster of palmetto. JD's head snapped back at the crack of the rifle and he fell to the ground beside Carter. A man rose from the cover and began a hasty retreat when both barrels of Bull's shotgun caught the bandit high in the back, lifting him from his feet and throwing him face-down among the weeds.

Jim cried out and ran to the old man's side and rolled him over to look into his eyes. Carter turned and reached for his uncle as the old man began to smile.

"I guess Carter was right. There was another one around." JD said softly then sat up with Jim's help and placed his hands firmly over the long bloody crease he now had over his left ear.

"You just be holdin' real still now, and let ol' Bull tend to ya'. Aw, it aint much more than a scratch my friend. A few days and a bit of rest and you'll be good as new." Bull was saying as he placed a makeshift bandage about the cattleman's head. Then turning to Carter asked him, "What was all that yelling you was doing back there? I thought for a moment you'd caught the devil by his tail and couldn't turn him loose."

Carter smiled weakly as he lay back on the ground and answered.

"That yelling, might have saved my life just then. I saw the fear on their faces and they couldn't hold their guns straight. It gave me an advantage. I learned that from General Jackson's boys, they called it the Rebel Yell."

"You be quiet now cousin." Jim spoke calmly and in a reassuring tone. "We'll be at the fort before sundown and there is a good doctor there, but you must focus on living. You've lost a lot of blood and we need you to stay strong. Can you do that?"

Carter nodded silently as Jim and Bull set to work on building the travois.

XV

The day was beginning to wane as the sun crept toward the horizon above the green waters of the Gulf of Mexico. Buford found this time of day to be the most comfortable as the trade winds blew in from over the water, cooling the little fort. He had stepped onto the porch of his little ramshackle office space and was enjoying a fine cigar while watching the evenings goings on at the forts compound. Most of the soldiers stationed there were inside the large dining hall off to the south end of the compound. leaving a few civilian inhabitants to carry on about their assigned chores before retiring for the evening. There were a few sentries posted about the fort, as always, but they bore their duties out of respect of the militaries attempt at maintaining regularity, not for necessity for the fort hadn't been under fire since the second Seminole war.

As he stood on the small porch, blowing rings in the smoke of his cigar, Buford noticed the gate sentry suddenly react and begin signaling for other soldiers to prepare for incoming riders. Very shortly thereafter, four horses entered the compound carrying three riders. The fourth horse had been pulling a sort of make shift sled, upon which lay a man obviously in need of a doctor.

One of the riders, a bare-chested Indian, assisted one of the others with a bandaged head, from his horse and ran toward the office of the fort's only physician. The other two gave their attention to the man on the sled. Buford stepped from the porch and started over to the men as soldiers streamed out to assist them when the man with the bandaged head stood up and turned so that Buford could identify him. It was JD Floydd!

He took note of the blood on the old mans hands and arms as well as the blood showing on the bandage as JD spoke with a young lieutenant from the fort's cavalry detachment and he returned to the porch to continue watching. Shortly after the doctor arrived, the men moved into the fort's crude hospital and a dozen or so of the fort's horse soldiers mounted up and rode out east along the cattle trail. Buford went inside and sat at his desk with his mind racing over turn of events. He had known that Alford was deadly serious in his determination to stop the cattleman from bringing in a herd, but somehow thoughts of bloodshed had never seemed real to Buford until now. Seeing the cattleman and his hands at the fort, Buford knew he was done and this could never end well for him at all.

Reaching inside the drawer of his desk, he produced a silver flask that had been a birthday gift long ago. He downed a quick shot of the bitter liquid it contained and sat smoking the cigar while miserably trying to decide upon a course of action for himself.

From the small windows of his office, he now could hear the sounds of cattle being gathered at the large stock pens just outside the fort's walls. Alford Kennedy would be out for blood and Clinton should be back in any day now. He considered turning himself over to the captain of the fort and take his chances, but the possibility of a prison sentence was too much for him to bear. Flight may be possible if he left immediately and it was possible to gain passage on a vessel leaving tonight. Suicide was certainly not an option, but to stay and face Kennedy may have the same results. Given the choices, Buford chose to flee. He packed furiously and ran to the room of a nearby hotel where his personal baggage was gathered and he made his way toward the docks.

Buford sat leaning against a hand rail on the dock and smoked another cigar while trying to understand how he'd let himself become so involved with this treacherous affair. He'd made arrangements to board a vessel leaving at first light of the morning for the panhandle and he decided to spend his night waiting there on the dock, rather than risk discovery in his hotel room.

He smoked and watched a tug boat, with an eight man crew bearing long oars, fight to position a small ship against the dock for unloading. A young boy made his way along the length of the dock, lighting lanterns on his way which cast their light out against the gathering shadows. A man walked up the dock from the direction of the warehouses and Buford didn't take particular notice of the burly figure until it stopped in front of him and spoke.

"Buford, what brings you out tonight? Are you hear to meet William back from St. Augustine?" Asked Alford Kennedy.

Buford looked up and fear clutched his throat, making him nearly choke on his reply.

"No, I wasn't aware he was due in tonight." He stammered.

"Well, that's his boat coming in now. Just why are you out here Buford and what about that luggage? You can't be leaving, we have to conclude our business with that ranch. Where do you think you're going?" Kennedy asked with rising concern.

Buford stood to face the man and with a sigh of resignation, told him the truth.

"There is no more business to conclude. JD Floydd recently arrived into the fort and has a herd penned up at the stock yard right now. He came in with some others and they've been shot up. It's over Alford, you didn't stop him and it's over. The whole fort will be out looking into who's responsible for all this and I don't plan on being anywhere around when they come looking my way." Buford told him resolutely.

A cold rage began to burn in the piggish eyes of Alford Kennedy and his cheeks began to flush a deep crimson.

"This can't be over you little bastard! There has to be something that you can do to fix this. I need that land and I need it now! What are you going to do to fix this?"

"I can't fix it!" Buford cried out in defeat. "I suggest that you get Clinton off of that boat and the two of you get on the very next one available and get out of here. You were supposed to stop them from selling those cows, but you didn't. Now there's two wounded men in the hospital and the cavalry already has set out to investigate how that happened. You blew this deal, not me and I can't fix it."

Alford looked around nervously then taking the little man's arm into his grasp, he led Buford over behind a large stack of crates that were piled high upon the docks waiting to be loaded aboard some ship or another.

"Listen to me!" Alford hissed venomously. "You will not walk away and leave us holding the bag! You will fix this or I will kill you, do you understand me?"

"I've already told you, I can't! I'm getting out while I can and I suggest you give up and do the same, now there's nothing more to discuss." Buford boldly answered and turned to leave.

He never saw the knife appear in the ham sized hand of the big man, nor did he see the arm thrust forward, but he did feel the blade as it sank deeply into his kidney. He tried to cry out in pain and fear, but couldn't draw the breath with which to shout. He turned again and looked into the wildly evil eyes of his former partner who caught him by the shirt front and lowered him to the wooden planks of the dock before withdrawing the knife, only to plunge it home again, just over the left nipple.

Buford closed his eyes and felt the cool smooth surface of the boards beneath him as his consciousness failed him and Buford Fetterman slipped away from the world forever.

XVI

As the travois bounced along behind the horse, Carter felt himself passing in and out of consciousness. Each time he would awaken, he would find that the pain had grown and he suffered along from an incredible thirst. He would try to ask for a drink, but the attempt to speak tired him so and he fell back into a dark sleep. One time Carter awoke to find himself being carried by men with faces he could not focus on and whose voices rang hollow and without familiarity. Another time he awoke while being held up while a man in a white frock placed bandages about his middle and introduced himself as a doctor. The doctor offered him water and Carter drank deeply. His head began to spin as the doctor talked on about blood loss and bandages before the sleep took him away again.

The next time he awoke, the room was dark and cool. Everything was quiet and he became a little disoriented. He started to rise up until a searing pain in his abdomen reminded him of his condition and memories of the days events slowly crawled around in his mind. Across the small room a small oil lamp was burning and he could make out the slender silhouette of someone slid down into a chair, possibly asleep.

"Can I have some water?" He asked in a dry crackling voice.

Shaking herself awake, Josephina got to her feet and came quickly to him.

"Carter?" She asked tenderly.

"I was wanting some water. Thirsty."

"Of course, I'll get it." She poured from a pitcher on a stand beside the bed and gently held his head as she placed the cool cup to his parched lips for him to drink. He sipped slowly at first then in great needy gulps. She refilled the cup two more times and when he'd drank all he could at the time, lowered his head back upon the pillow and wiped the excess from his chin.

"Where am I at?" Carter asked her weakly.

"We're at the fort, in the hospital. You've been here for a day and a half now. You've been sleeping."

"How did you get here?"

"I got in last evening. You're uncle didn't want you to be alone, so he asked Jim to bring me here to you. The doctor says that the bullet didn't hurt your insides and only busted up one of your ribs. He said that your going to be fine after all, but that you lost quite a lot of blood and that you'll be needing time to get stronger. As soon as you do, I'll help you back to the ranch in the wagon. But there's no rush. I expect your gonna be one sore fellow for awhile." She spoke tenderly.

"What about JD, I saw him get hit. Is he going to be okay?"

"He's just fine. The bullet left a pretty good sized gash over his left ear, but it only grazed him. The doctor put a few stitches in it to be safe. You all were very lucky. The cattle made it in and have already been sold. The captain here at the fort is sending the money ahead on to the tax office in Washington DC himself since Mr. Fetterman was found dead."

"The tax man?" Carter asked confused.

"Yes, he was murdered over on the docks. The two men that he was helping, apparently the ones that sent those men against you, left aboard a sailing ship yesterday morning, just before his body was found behind some crates." She explained.

"What happens now?"

"The ship they boarded is bound for Appalachicola Bay and the Captain has already telegraphed ahead to the US Marshall's office and they'll have someone there to meet them when the ship arrives."

Carter just shook his head and closed his eyes, letting her words sink in.

"There's more to tell, but nothing that can't wait until morning. But, Carter, I've heard all about what happened out there and how if it hadn't been for your help, I don't know what would have become of us all. I want you to rest now and heal so I can bring you home." She told him then leaned over and kissed his cheek.

"What was that for?" He asked in surprise.

"Because I wanted to kiss you. I hope you don't mind." She said a little embarrassed.

"Josephina, I don't mind. I've wanted to be kissed by you since the other night when I heard you singing to your pony." He admitted.

Even in the darkness of the room, he could tell she was blushing, then she leaned over and kissed him full on the lips.

"Is that what you had in mind?" She asked as she took his hand in hers.

"That's right, and a whole lot more of them." He said, wearing a thin smile.

XVII

He rested his horse in the shade of a small oak grove growing along the western edge of a small pasture his uncle had cleared of palmetto and scrub a good many years ago. He was waiting for Bull and one of the Seminoles his uncle hired as cowboys to help with the spring roundup. They were making a short drive through a cane break along the rivers edge. He himself had gathered a small herd and they had settled nicely into the pasture feeding quietly on the new grasses. As he waited, he rubbed his horses neck and spoke softly to the animal.

"You did good this morning ol' Boy. I know it's hot out there, but we're almost done for today. Just a bit more to go and we can both go and get some rest. Whattaya say Gator? That sound good to you?"

JD had given him the horse after the drive to the fort, although it had been a few weeks before Carter was able to ride again. The doctor had told him he'd be sore for awhile and he was right. The wound healed up quickly enough, but even six weeks later, if Carter moved wrong, his ribs would reward him with a sharp, stabbing pain.

They stood there together, Carter and his horse, for a good hour or more until he saw the first cows begin to drift into the far end of the little pasture ahead of his fellow riders. He stepped into the stirrup with a grunt of pain and swung himself into the saddle. They moved into the sunlight and Carter cracked his new whip a couple of times to get his herds attention. He slowly got his herd moving and was soon joined by the dozen or so gathered by Bull and his Seminole companion Egret. The three riders directed them south along the cattle trail leading toward the catch pens near the ranch house.

Bull rode in close to Carter and reported on the drive while wiping his sweat and dust covered forehead with his sweaty, dusty shirt sleeve.

"They's nothing left behind us but steers. These are the only calves and she stuff in sight. It's not a small herd though. That should keep the boy's busy for a time eh?"

"There aint but forty or so calves in the whole bunch here. I expect they'll have this bunch done by lunchtime tomorrow, so we'd best spend the morning checking the cattail marshes on the river to the east. I bet we find a few head hiding in there from the heat." Carter replied with a good natured smile.

"Egret was telling me that this is the best spring roundup JD's had in a long time. Aint that so young fella?" Bull called out to the young Indian.

"It's true, we have many more calves than in the past. The bulls must have been busy during the winter. I've worked many springs for your uncle so I remember. He will be pleased." Egret answered, proud to have been asked.

"I wonder how Josephina and Paulo are doing on their drive along Lost Dog Creek?" Carter asked neither of them directly.

"Probably the same as we are. JD rode through there yesterday and said that there was plenty of cattle there." Egret answered him, then Bull cut in for the tease.

"Carter, is it the calves your worrying about, or are you jealous?" He asked grinning, which pulled a knowing chuckle from the Seminole.

"That's not what I was askin' at all. I was wonderin' about the roundup's all." Carter fired back.

"Surely Lad, that pretty eyed cowpoke had nothing to do with it." Bull agreed with a sarcastic wink which brought another chuckle from Egret.

"Well I will say this." Carter responded defensively. "She'd sure beat looking at you two all day long."

"Yes, and I can only guess at the herd you two would gather alone. I bet you wouldn't find a cow at all for looking after each other." Egret joined in the ribbing, his comment breaking Bull into a hearty laugh and he rode over and slapped Carter good naturedly on his back.

"Well, go on and laugh you two, I can take it. She just weighs on my mind is all." Carter admitted, a little embarrased, his cheeks tinged red, but grinning from ear to ear at his good humored companions.

"We've all been there Carter." Bull told him with his hand still out on Carter's shoulder and their horses touching. "It's love that keeps us young. I know I've felt it more than once in my past, that's for sure."

The cows exited the small pasture and began to spread out over a low growing palmetto flats and the riders split up to guide the cattle together along a dim trail, back toward the catch pens. The noon day sun had been beating down from a cloudless sky and battered down upon the drovers, making any conversation end quickly. The mornings breeze had long ago halted and the dust kicked up from the cattle's hooves upon the trail, rose straight up around them. Sweat had long ago broken out upon the bodies of the men and mixing with the dust, created a gritty film which completely coated them in a most uncomfortably gritty way.

They pushed the cattle beneath scattered pines toward a flat topped hill that marked the location of the ranches corral. As the drivers approached, Carter could see that it held a large herd already and he quickly spotted Josephina leaning on a fence railing, talking with JD. Her pony was picketed outside of the pen and she looked to be about as dirty as he was himself. It took a lot of help to get the herds mixed within the holding pen, but eventually the gate was shut and Carter dismounted to join Josephina and his uncle outside the pen.

"How many do you think are there all together?" Carter asked.

"About two hundred and thirty." Josephina answered. "How was your day, did you have any trouble?"

"No, I'm fine. I'm pretty sore from all of the bouncing in the saddle, but I'll be fine. How about you?"

"No trouble at all. They rounded up as sweet as kittens." Josephina assured him.

JD had stepped up on a fence railing and was making several fast motions of his right hand over the herd with his fingers spread wide. In a moment, he stepped down and looked at Josephina with a broad grin.

"That's some good countin' girl. That's two hundred and thirty head on the nose." He complimented her. "That's a good gathering for the first day. Startin' tomorrow, we'll get to brandin' and castratin' while the boys sweep out and find us some more. What do you think Carter?"

"Suits me fine, I had planned to round up some more tomorrow though." Carter told him.

"I know, but I want you here. You'll get plenty of work, but you'll be out of the saddle for awhile. Maybe we can give your ribs some more time to heal."

"Whatever you say." Carter agreed. "If we're done for the day now, we'd best head toward the house. I think Josephina's gonna need to wash up before supper."

JD gave a laugh and Josephina punched his shoulder in mock anger then told him.

"I wouldn't talk to much about needing a bath mister. You look like you've been rolling in the dirt with your horse. Momma Luanne is gonna have to feed you out on the porch or she'll never get all of your dirt out of the house after you walk in like that."

Grinning, he took her by the hand and they started off toward the horses together.

XVIII

After breakfast had settled comfortably in their bellies the next morning, the crew had found their way toward the split railed corral holding the previous days gathering of cows and calves. On one side of the structure was a narrow shoot through which the cattle could exit one at a time. Near by that opening was a waist high pile of wood beside which JD sat about building a fire to heat the three branding irons he'd brought along for the days work.

Josephina and Bull headed off together to gather more calves and Paulo and a couple of Seminole's headed off in another direction seeking the same. JD, Carter and the young Seminole Egret stayed at the corral to handle the herd. First Carter and Egret began separating the cows from their calves inside the corral while trying to turn the cows into the exit shoot leaving the calves behind.

Luanne rode up shortly after they began in the buckboard wagon from which JD grabbed a couple of large sacks containing sulfur powder that was used to dust all of the cows as they were allowed to exit the shoot. The sulfur dust, Luanne explained to Carter, was to help the cows fend off the ever present horde of flies and tick which plagued them during the hotter months. Once the cows were dusted and removed from the corral, JD checked to be sure that the irons were hot enough and signaled Egret to begin bringing calves out, one at a time.

Egret rode his horse slowly toward the bunched calves. They split apart at his approach and tried their best to avoid him. He picked a calf on the outside of the group, moved in behind it and snaked a small loop on the ground in front of its hind legs. The calf took the step into it and Egret jerked up the slack. Holding the rope taught he turned his horse and came away at a slow trot, draggin' the bawling animal backwards on its belly. After he had drug it through and cleared the shoot, Carter shut the gate and grabbed the calf as it struggled back to its feet.

JD called out to Carter, "You take the tail and I'll grab the rope. When I say, we'll flip him over and you hold him down. Put your left knee in his neck and pull up on a foreleg so that he can't get up."

"Now!" He shouted and yanked hard on the rope.

Uncertain, Carter pulled the tail without much effect. The calf staggered a bit, but remained on its feet.

JD chuckled, "It's timing son, you have to pull up at the exact time that I do and we'll use the calf's weight against him. Now, pull!"

Carter yanked on the tail strongly at the same time as JD pulled the rope in the opposite direction. The calf flopped over on its side with its back toward Carter. He quickly mounted the calf and on the second try managed to grip the foreleg and he held the bawling calf down. Luanne handed JD an iron with which he stamped on a B3C brand on the calf's flank. White smoke curled up from the calf's hide with a hiss, attacking Carter's nostrils. Just then Luanne stepped in and JD held the tail up as she expertly turned the young bull calf into a steer. She daubed some dark stinky paste over the new incision and stepped around Carter to place a notch in the calf's left ear. Afterward, she stepped back and JD gave Carter the order to release it.

"Okay Son, you can let this one go. Here comes Egret with another." His uncle gave him a quick smile and a wink.

Carter soon learned that throwing the calves was easy if he coordinated his move with JD's. In fact he found that he enjoyed matching his strength against the weight of the animals regardless of the dull ache that it created in his still healing ribs. Egret timed his roping and dragging to keep them busy all morning at a steady pace. By the time JD called break, they had gone through more than two thirds of the calves.

Luanne set out a cold lunch of hard tack and boiled a huge pot of coffee over the branding fire. They sat in the shade of the little wagon and downed their lunch with little conversation. It seemed a bit hot out to be drinking coffee, but to Carter, it never tasted better. He took notice of JD as he sat with his back against the wagons wheel not eating. The old man caught Carter's eye and he looked away and began to rise. Once he had gained his footing JD staggered a little and Carter jumped to his own feet, with growing alarm.

"JD, are you doing all right?"

"Oh yeah. I'm fine, don't worry about me none. I've got quite a ways to go before I'm worn out."

"Maybe you'd better take a break for a while longer. You don't need to push yourself. These beeves are gonna get taken care of in good time." Carter offered to him.

Luanne stepped up to her husband and placed her hand on his sleeve and spoke to him with real concern in her eyes.

"Are you sure your okay? If you need to rest then do it! I don't want your heart to act up. You remember that doctor said for you to be taking it easy when you can."

"Well," he began to give in. "How's about I ride the horse awhile and do the roping? There's not any strain in that and Egret can help Carter throw and brand the calves, if he don't mind."

"I won't mind at all as long as it's only the calves that he uses that branding iron on." He nodded to Carter with a grin as he stepped over to the wagon to deposit his empty plate.

"Let's get back to work then." JD told them as he headed toward the horse. "They'll be arriving with a new bunch in just a few hours and I'd really like to get through with as many as we can. It'd be best to get that corral all the way empty before they get here, so we might as well get to it." He said as he swung up into the saddle with a grunt.

The afternoon sun had slipped halfway toward the horizon before the sound of cracking whips alerted the crew at the corral another herd was being delivered. Carter didn't mind the interruption in his work as he stopped long enough to prepare the corral to receive the new arrivals. The constant aching in his ribs was not as bad as usual as he moved about the corral and he felt proud of the work he'd done, but a deep concern for his Uncle built within him as he noticed the old man slouching in the saddle.

"JD, we're about done here for the day. Way I see it, you and Aunt Luanne may as well head on for the house. We'll settle this bunch coming in and when the others arrive, we'll put them to bed and come on to the house ourselves." Carter suggested to his uncle.

"He's right Old Man." Luanne broke in. "You come along now. I drew you a fresh bath this morning before I came out and I think a cool bath will do you some good."

"I don't know what you two are so worried about me for." JD said straightening himself up and giving them a look of reproach.

"I feel as good now as I ever had in my whole life, but I might just as well go get that bath if you youngun's think you can handle it from here on out. Just, if you will, when Josephina comes in, send her along to the house to give Luanne a bit of help with preparing tonight's victuals. I'll see ya'll at the house tonight then." He told them and started his horse over to where Carter's aunt was starting her little wagon back over the trail.

Paulo, the big shoeless Seminole, and his two companions were the first to arrive in with about two dozen head of cows and calves. After gathering the newly acquired herd into the corral with the remainders of yesterdays roundup, Carter decided to continue with the branding until Josephina and Bull arrived. Egret roped another calf and brought it out bawling and struggling. Carter jumped on the animal and struggled at first with the calf's supple hide slipping through his fingers until he got a firm grip on the calf's neck and another hand under its flank and wrestled the writhing critter to the ground. Carter found it decidedly harder to throw a calf by himself. Sweat stung his eyes and his throat clogged with dust as he held the kicking calf while Paulo walked over and applied the brand of the B3C. Carter loosened his grip and the tormented heifer broke free to go and find it's mother.

"That was some wrastlin' Carter. I guess you haven't done this before, huh?" Paulo asked him with a grin.

"Just this mornin' with JD is all." Carter admitted, a little embarrassed by the fumbling.

"Here, you take the irons and I'll throw the next one to show you how it's done, all right?" Paulo asked him.

"Sounds good to me." Carter agreed and then called to Egret, "Bring us another one, Paulo's going to give me some lessons."

Egret complied and soon another calf made its way through the shoot behind his horse and no sooner had it regained its feet that Paulo threw himself on the calf as it made a jump and used the calf's own momentum to throw it. He made it look easy enough and Carter stepped in and branded the young bull, then taking out his knife, repeated the surgery he'd seen his aunt performing all morning and made his first steer.

Before Egret brought out another though, he alerted them that the other herd was coming into view and that they should get ready to receive them. Josephina and Bull were riding behind a fair sized bunch about a half of a mile out when Carter rode out to meet them.

"Don't come ridin' out here now, tryin' to drive in this herd Lad." Bull called out to him as he drew near. "We've driven these darn cows all this way by ourselves and we're apt to get them the rest of the way too. I should've figured you to come help at this stage. I think I'll start callin' you blister." He finished with a smile.

"Now why would you want to call me that?" Carter asked in amusement.

"Because like a blister, you seem to be the first thing to show up after the work is done." He replied grinning.

"Ha! I guess I been workin' all day myself. JD's done got plenty of sweat outta me today."

"I hope you didn't over do it." Josephina cut in. "If your not too worn out, I might want you to take me swimming by the river tonight. Maybe we can wash off some of this dirt." She told him in a teasing tone and offering a mischievous smile upon her dirt streaked face.

"I just might, but right now, you'd best high tail it on up to the house. JD's not feelin' too good and he's got me worried. He didn't put up to much of a fight when we suggested he head on back and he said to send you on up when you get in to help Aunt Luanne with supper."

"When did he get sick?" She asked seriously.

"He sort of went downhill right after lunch. He had been helping me throw and brand the calves and he got a bit too hot I think. He stayed on for awhile though and roped some on horseback until Paulo's herd came in, then he let us finish up today. He left with Aunt Luanne about an hour and a half ago."

"Then I'd better get. I'll meet ya'll back at the house." She walked her little horse forward and leaned way over to give Carter a quick kiss before spurring the little pony homeward.

"Poor fellow." Bull sighed.

"Oh, he'll be fine Bull. He just got too hot." Carter said reassuringly.

"I wasn't talking about JD. You're the one whose missing out on the skinny dip." Bull let out with a hearty laugh. "Come now Lad. Let's get this herd penned." He was still laughing at his own joke as he cracked his whip and moved forward behind the cows.

Carter fell in beside him red faced and grinning.

Just before sundown Carter rode up to the house with Bull, Paulo and Egret in tow. Bull offered to take Gator on into the stables and put him up for the night so that Carter could get inside and check on JD, so he dismounted and Bull took up the reins and led the cow pony on back to the barn. Carter stepped up to the porch and cleaned up as best he could from the wash basin his aunt had left out for them and then he came on inside to find JD seated at the dinner table holding a steaming crockery mug of coffee. It was apparent that he had taken advantage of the bath Luanne had fixed for him and although his color was still a bit gray, he looked as if he had mostly shaken off his infirmities from earlier.

"JD, you look like your feeling better. I guess Aunt Luanne's tub bath did you some good." Carter said trying not to sound worried.

"Yeah, that cool water sure does the trick to cool a man off."

"Just got a little too hot eh?" Carter asked.

"Yep, don't worry about me. I'm ready to go again." JD told him .

"I don't doubt it. But, I was wanting to make sure it weren't your heart." Carter said softly while looking into the gray eyes of the old cattleman.

"I appreciate you being worried, but don't. I've already received my sermons from Luanne first and then Josephine when she came in." The old man waved his hand toward

Carter and let out a chuckle. "Now I'm afraid I can't even pass gas without one of them wantin' to know if I'm okay."

"They love you. They're supposed to worry."

"I know. What bothers me really is that I've given them a reason to be worried. I guess I'm learnin' what bein' an old man's all about. There aint much I can do about it either, time just keeps marching along. But, old or not, there's still work around here that has to be tended too and I'm not gonna have folks out there sweatin' on my behalf whilst I sit up on the porch in a rocker. No Sir! I just have to learn to pace myself, that's all."

Carter pulled out a chair and took a seat across from his uncle.

"You know, JD. A couple of more days and we'll be pretty well done with all this roundup. The way I figure, If you'll do the ropin' and draggin', Egret and Me'll do the rest. We worked good together today and we'll go through them calves in no time."

"Sounds good, but you have to take it easy yourself. I wouldn't want anything bustin' loose inside you from them ribs. How you holdin' up today anyhow?" JD asked, turning the tables

"I am pretty sore, but I'll rub down good with lineament before I turn in. I'm learnin' how to move so as not to hurt myself." Carter assured him then asked, "Where are the ladies tonight?"

"They're both in the kitchen out back. Josephine took a quick bath and run out to help with the cookin'." His uncle told him and then with a shrewd look coming over him said, "I been noticin' the way you two been actin' around each other for some time now. I hadn't wanted to bring it up and say anything, but what are you planning to do about it?"

"Do about it?" Carter repeated the question, completely caught off guard.

"I'm sorry for bringing it up at all Carter, but I'm kinda her dad now, you know?"

"I know." He said recovering from the shock. "I've been studyin' on that very thing and I'd like to ask her to marry me. I been meanin' to talk to you about it for awhile now." Carter nervously admitted.

"I've seen it comin' and Luanne and I have talked on it a bit. Just hear me out on this. I'm not tellin' you to run to the preacher, you two take care of that with our blessings in your own time. It's just that if you do marry, then we'd like to ask you to build your home right here on the ranch. I know I haven't any right to ask that of you since you might want to head back to Georgia and farm with your brother, but we've grown right fond of you Son and your leavin' would be bad enough, but if Josephina was to light out as well; well it'd tear the heart right out of us. Do you understand Carter?" The old man asked sincerely and honest.

"Uncle JD, I plan to ask her and if she'll have me, I can't think of any place else in the world I would want to be than right here. After the war ended and I came home to all that I did, I wasn't sure that I would ever find a place that I could feel at home, but you and Aunt Luanne have given that back to me. I miss Seth, but I feel like I belong here and I thank you for that. I really do." Carter finished with unfeigned gratitude.

"Good. Very good!" JD spoke with a grin spreading across his face and he reached across the table to offer Carter his hand.

Carter took his uncle's hand in a firm grip and with an honest shake, began his future on the B3C.

About the Author

Toby Benoit is a native Floridian with a love of his home state and its history. He was raised on a small farm in a rural community and has went on to lead a life full of diversity and achievement. Professionally he has enjoyed success as a family counselor in the funeral industry, an expert in the archery/bowhunting industry and as a geriatric nurse/ therapist. Now at age thirty-four, Toby is a notable freelance columnist for several outdoor sporting magazines and part-time novelist.

Toby is a Christian and a mason whose recreational pastimes include hunting, fishing, farming, turkey call making and archery. He lives in Citrus county Florida surrounded by family, friends and Tank. His Jack Russell terrier.

Printed in the United States
21234LVS00001B/392